A Dragon, Some Whiskey, and People

A Collection of Short Stories

Shawn Jolley

Contents

Introduction

When I was growing up, before I learned how to write, I learned how to read. I fell in love with stories early on. Some of the books that I enjoyed reading were short story collections.

For the most part, the genres I read were horror and mystery. Partially, because of the limited selection of books in my school library and partially because of my own love of monsters, whodunits, and the supernatural.

On occasion, I would grab a fantasy or general fiction compilation.

I remember reading a short story in grade school about an overweight loner of a man who had a large and vicious mouth in place of his stomach. That bit wasn't particularly scary. The scary part was how he used his extra mouth to eat neighborhood children, and it was always in extremely descriptive detail.

When I finished the story—and it didn't have a happy ending—I felt sick. Unfortunately, that wasn't all. The story gave me nightmares for a week. I'm still not sure if the librarian knew about the graphic nature of the book when she gave it to me.

Either way, I learned that the magic of good fiction is that it sticks with you for years. Notice that fifteen years later I have forgotten the title of the short story but not how it made me feel. In fact, I wouldn't be one bit surprised if I had a dream tonight that involved the loner man with his stomach mouth.

Now that I've grown up, I've started to write my own short stories, and I still love to read them. In fact, at the time of writing this, I'm working my way through two short story collections. One of them is comprised of mostly mysteries while the other is made up of suspenseful (and somewhat horrific) thrillers.

A Dragon, Some Whiskey, and People is my first short story collection. The eleven stories that appear in this book originally debuted on my blog. I placed them in this collection for the benefit of my readers.

My hope is that by creating this book, in both physical and digital formats, my stories will be able to reach anyone who wants to read them. May you enjoy them as much as I do.

One

Old Oaks

WHAT THE HOUSE REALLY needed was a wrecking ball and a few dozen sticks of dynamite. The location, in a remote corner of the Colorado Rockies, might have been great for a bed-and-breakfast, but it was useless because the road leading up to it was more like a hiking trail than anything else.

There was a town five miles to the south, but the small community, consisting mostly of abandoned mobile homes, wasn't a place people visited by choice.

The truth was, the house, although Victorian in style and large enough to accommodate the biggest of families, had been doomed since the first nail had been hammered into the first board. The original builder, one Arthur B. Kingkiller according to the faded plaque next to the front door, obviously hadn't cared about resale value, much to the disappointment of many modern investors. He wanted the house to be built in the middle of nowhere, and so it was.

The outside of the house was supposed to be white, but the paint had chipped in large and small chunks, revealing dark and rough rotting wood. Rain gutters gilded in rust clung to the edges in an attempt to remain part of the structure. Shingles littered the flower beds where plants should have been growing.

Having been unoccupied for forty-two years, the neglect and misery manifested themselves in every man-made piece of the scene. Even the surrounding trees looked unnatural in juxtaposition to the broken home. The rumor was that somebody, or something, more than likely dead, still roamed the hallways, stood in the rooms, and watched the road from the shattered windows.

Nobody knew if the rumors were true, only that they had started with the mysterious disappearance of the previous homeowners. The county police department still had the original report that was filed on the night Mr. and Mrs. Kingkiller left town, but the facts were vague.

At the time, the Kingkillers had been in the process of moving west for more employment opportunities (the local mine having shut down), but they had left earlier than they had said they would. This, coupled with the fact that there had been traces of blood near the house's front entrance, along with some teeth, made the whole county uneasy.

Despite the evidence, there had been no weapon, and there had never been a hint of motive. Without any further evidence, including bodies, anything pointing to foul play was deemed null by the police department.

In fact, the people from the area say there was never a proper investigation, but that everything had been swept under the rug.

As the years passed, urban legends took the place of truth. Lights were seen in the windows, music was heard down the road. Hunters claimed there wasn't a deer, bear, or wild goat within fifteen miles of the place.

The house hadn't changed much over the preceding decades, aside from the natural wear and tear of abandonment. The same oak trees surrounded the backside of the house; their leaves changing color the same way they did every autumn.

Early in the year, during the spring and summer months, the constant warbling of blackbirds, swallows, owls, and brown creepers who nested in the woods filled the air.

On this day, there were no songs, but two blue jays flew overhead, apparently ready to find warmer weather elsewhere. The two birds went unnoticed by two teenagers, a boy and a girl, walking hand in hand on the lone mountain road that led to the house.

Shay stopped walking when she saw the house, a dizzying sort of feeling having spread through her head. She closed her eyes, took a deep breath, and zipped her jacket up with her free hand. Her boyfriend, Aaron, stopped beside her and glanced over.

"Are you all right?" he asked.

"Yeah, I'm fine. You?"

Aaron hesitated for a moment. "Couldn't be better." He squeezed Shay's hand. "Are you ready for your surprise?"

"Of course I'm ready. I've been thinking about it all week." She smiled unconvincingly and scrunched up her nose. Aaron shook his head.

"I thought your stomach was feeling better," he said. "Why don't you sit down for a minute?" He helped Shay to the ground. "Do you think it's the burrito fiesta casserole?" he asked while smiling.

Shay laughed. "Probably. School lunch sucks." She leaned against Aaron as he rubbed her back.

A man dressed almost entirely in spandex jogged past the two of them with a courtesy smile and nod. A dog followed closely behind the man with its tongue hanging to the side of its mouth. Shay thought she recognized the jogger but couldn't remember where she had seen him.

"Who was that?" she asked.

"Who?" asked Aaron, looking around.

"Who do you think? The man who just passed us with his dog."

Aaron raised his eyebrows and waited for a punchline, but when it didn't come, he changed the subject. "We can do this another time," he said.

Shay dropped the subject of the man and his dog. "No, I'm good. Come on." She stood up, trying her best to look healthy and happy.

Aaron took her hand without question. They walked up to the house together. It looked much bigger up close than it had from the road.

Shay's stomach pain lessened as they approached the front porch, (the burrito fiesta casserole apparently having settled) and she became genuinely excited.

"You're positive you're ready for your surprise?" asked Aaron. He had turned to stand between the door and Shay.

She nodded her head and looked over his shoulder. The door was old and faded, but it looked like it weighed a lot.

"You're not scared, are you?" Aaron moved his head back into Shay's line of sight.

"No," she said with a giggle. "Should I be?"

Aaron didn't laugh. "I don't know. Maybe." His face had gone pale.

"Are you scared?" she asked. She lifted her hand to his face and started moving her thumb in circles across his red, stubbly beard.

Aaron shook his head away from her hand. "Nervous."

Shay was about to ask what Aaron had to be nervous about when she noticed three large bullet holes in the center of the front door. She stepped around Aaron and poked the holes. Looking back, she said, "These are old, right?"

"Yeah," said Aaron, nodding. "It was probably just a bored hunter passing through." He pushed the front door open; it creaked on its hinges.

"Spooky," said Shay. Aaron chuckled.

The living room was cleaner than Shay thought it would be, although it was extremely dark. Two small windows near the ceiling let in a few rays of light. The hardwood floor had warped in several places and was covered in a thin layer of dust.

Broken furniture, (which Shay found exquisite nonetheless) had been pushed up against the sides of the room. A staircase on the far side of the room led to the second story.

Shay tried not to react when she noticed rose petals on the floor leading to the staircase.

Aaron smiled and kissed her. "Wait here just a moment," he said.

"Where are you going?"

"To get things ready." Aaron winked and went upstairs. Shay listened to the wooden steps groan under his weight.

The silence that followed was unbearable. She may have been anxious because of the pending surprise or because the house was simply too big, old, and empty. Either way,

Shay felt like she wasn't a welcome addition to the lonely space.

Five minutes turned into ten and still, Shay waited in the living room. She softly hummed her favorite song—Blackbird—but with each passing moment, she became more anxious.

"What if something is wrong?" she thought to herself. The house was old: maybe he fell through the floor, or maybe an old chandelier fell on him, or...

"Aaron," she called out.

No answer.

Shay walked to the bottom of the staircase and repeated herself; there was still no answer. Her heart sped up, and she began to sweat. She saw that the door at the top of the stairs was open a crack. "I hope he won't be angry," she thought.

The stairs squeaked rather than groaned as she climbed to the second floor. "Is everything okay?" she asked at the top of the stairs. Aaron didn't answer, but a voice boomed through Shay's head:

"He's mine!"

Shay grabbed the railing to keep herself from falling. "I'm going crazy," she thought. She took a few deep breaths and waited for something to happen, but nothing did. "I just need to get Aaron and get out of here."

She pushed the door open and sighed with relief. Aaron was standing in the hallway. He was turned away from her.

"There you are," she said. "Can we get out of here?"

Aaron turned around. His eyes, black; his face, pale. Dark blood trickled down his chin and neck. His mouth opened and Shay gasped. He had no teeth. His gums were raw and red. The veins in his neck visibly throbbing.

"Aaron," whispered Shay.

He took a step forward and moaned. A white vapor rose out of his mouth and dissipated.

"What's happened to you?"

He looked away for a moment then pulled a rusty hammer out from behind his back. He smiled a bloody smile.

"What're you doing?" screamed Shay. "It's me!" She took a step back.

The hammer, already covered in blood, looked dark and rigid. It swayed in Aaron's grip.

"He's mine!" the voice boomed again. This time, Shay fell backward down the steps and hit her head at the bottom. She looked up, disoriented, at the form making its way down the stairs.

"No, no, no," thought Shay. She got to her feet despite her hazy vision and parched throat and made a dash to the front door.

The sun had set and a chill filled the air. Footsteps sounded from the street and the jogger from earlier and his husky came into view.

"Help!" screamed Shay.

The jogger came over to her. "What's going on?" he asked.

"My boyfriend. He's inside. He needs help. There was a hammer, and I don't know." Shay burst into tears, and the man couldn't get anything else out of her. He walked past her to the front door. His husky stayed with Shay and quietly whined.

"Hello," the man called out. "Is anybody in there?"

There wasn't an answer.

The man looked back at Shay and pierced his lips. "This better not be a prank or something," he said. She barely heard him.

The man entered the house while Shay and the husky looked on. Shay scrunched her eyebrows and gasped. The jogger's voice had sounded just like the booming voice.

Five minutes passed before the jogger came out again. "That house is empty," he said.

Shay didn't respond.

"I don't know what you've gotten yourself into, but you're coming with me."

Shay placed her hands on the man's shoulders. "Who are you?" she asked.

"My name's Nick. Listen, we should go." He raised his hands to grab Shay's arms, but she dropped them quickly to her sides. She began walking down the road.

"Hey, where are you going? You don't have to leave," said Nick. "I have a phone. I'll just call for someone to come get you. To make sure you're alright? No? Why not? Hey, what's the matter?"

Shay had begun crying.

Nick sighed. "Look, I'll stay here with you for as long as you need." Shay nodded slowly, and Nick bent down to pet his dog.

After Shay composed herself, she bent down and gave her companions a hug. Nick hugged her back and his husky's tail wagged. "What's your dog's name?" she asked.

"Oh, I should have introduced you by now. I would like you to meet my best friend, Mary." Mary licked Shay's face enthusiastically.

"Mary," said Shay. She stared at the front door and wondered if the night had been real. "You mean, 'Mary,' as in Mary Kingkiller," she said. An image of a framed photograph hanging in the front room of the house flashed through Shay's mind: Arthur and Mary Kingkiller.

As she thought this, she turned and her eyes caught a glimpse of the upstairs window. Staring back at her was the face of Aaron. The perfect face with perfect teeth, perfect blue eyes, and perfect red hair. He was wearing a suit, standing perfectly still, watching her. Shay collapsed without a sound. The apparition in the window disappeared.

Nick let Shay's body fall to the ground. Mary barked once and wagged her tail.

The following morning, the abandoned house looked the same as it ever had. Nobody would know just by looking at it that it wasn't quite as empty as it had been the day before.

Two

Dining with the Dead

DEATH WAS NEARBY WHEN Roy seated himself at the head of the long dining room table. He sat there so he could see the open hallway door, for if the door was ever shut, it would make the dining room too small, and Roy was afraid that the smallness would drive him mad.

Truth be told, he wasn't sure why he was afraid of the door—what was on the other side—and he didn't know if he could ever overcome his fear. Every night, he tried to move on; and, every night, he thought he got a little closer to success.

The legs of Roy's chair scratched the wooden floor as he scooted himself closer to the table. Now comfortable, he leaned forward, placing his elbows on the table.

The table itself was a dark wood that had been recently dusted and set for dinner. Ornate bowls, cups, and plates had been placed neatly in front of each chair. The middle of the table was empty, waiting to be filled at any moment with fancy dishes of food.

Beautiful and old, arched windows set high up on the west wall let sunlight stream into the room. Dust could be seen swirling near the panes of glass in contrast to the gray brick walls. There were no other light sources. This was because the castle had never been updated with electricity since its building three hundred and seventy-two years prior to the invention of the light bulb. Even so, there had never been a need for an internal light until after the sunset. The builders had understood how to utilize the sun's rays until darkness fell.

Roy had been looking forward to eating dinner with his extended family, which was quite large. Unlike most men in their early twenties, he adored spending time with his family, from his cousins—no matter how many times removed—to his great aunts and uncles.

Unfortunately, it seemed to Roy that his family members led too busy of lives, which meant they weren't around often enough. However, when they did manage to get together for a meal, it was a treat to his soul, even if it was only for a short time. Being near family had always caused him to feel warm and happy: a feeling that was short-lived at all other moments. Friends and acquaintances did little to cheer his typically depressing demeanor. In his eyes, blood was, and always would be, thicker than water. He prided himself on these traditional values.

Roy blinked for the first time since sitting down, realizing that he had been lost in thought. He stared down the table in shock; he was the only person in the room. He frowned and wondered where everybody had gone to?

His hands lowered so that he could see the empty room more clearly. The door which led into the hallway was still open; nobody had shut it, which was good. He scrunched up his eyebrows and tried to remember what had happened just before dinner. His mind was frustratingly blank. The only part he was sure of was that nobody had said goodbye to him. As he continued to sit and think, the empty table stared back at him as only an inanimate object can.

A few minutes passed. His head rolled back slightly so that it rested fully on his shoulders and he began laughing hysterically. It was a single laugh that sounded as though it were composed of several laughs, with low tones and high tones. Spittle flew from his lips and his open eyes rolled back into his skull. He had not laughed this hard in a long, long time.

The laughter bounced around the room, filled every corner, and flooded into the hallway. The dust particles moved faster as they passed the window panes. The sunlight changed color, from bright yellow to soft red. Echoes of laughter compounded as the lone diner began crying and wheezing. Everyone had simply left, and it was too funny.

Shortly before the sunset, the laughing fit passed, and Roy looked back down at the table. It was no longer empty; and, upon realizing this, he smiled. In fact, the table was now crowded with relatives: the chairs filled. Everyone in the room stared at Roy and smiled. They looked eager to eat.

Roy saw no reason to delay the meal any longer. He only wished that he had a mirror to check his appearance, as he felt sweaty and tired.

Bones—human skeletons—sat in the chairs. Many of the skulls had cracks running along the forehead or through the jawbone. Here, an arm was missing, there, a leg was gone. Spiders with their cobwebs crawled through the white, open spaces. A few earwigs could be seen wiggling along the surface of the table. The dying sunlight was now a hazy purple. The bones themselves looked dry and brittle.

At long last, the last of the echoing laughter died away. Roy stared at the open hallway door. He grabbed an empty wine glass from in front of him and raised it. Sitting up straight in his chair, upon clearing his throat, he began to speak. As he spoke, his eyes shone brightly. Before too long, he finished and put the wineglass down. Fifteen steps later, the hallway door closed, and the dining room was left without life.

Three

A Horse Broke Free

WHILE AVOIDING THE BLACK Death and ignoring King Edward III, a three-member merchant's guild traveled through a dense forest on their way to an isolated town southwest of The Wash on the eastern side of England. They walked in silence since the leader of the guild, Actius, preferred the sounds of nature to human companionship.

It was late afternoon on a surprisingly warm autumn day, considering it had rained the night before. The majority of the puddles in the road had dried early in the day.

The miserable trio ran into trouble shortly before noon when a rustling noise coming from the woods spooked their only horse. There was a flurry of movement accompanied by the trio's simultaneous exclamations of alarm. Hardly a moment passed before the horse broke free from its restraints. Leather straps and wood bits fell to the road. The merchants yelled for the horse to come back but its tail disappeared behind a bend in the road.

The growing distance between the cart and the animal drowned out the hoof beats. Seconds later, a squirrel ran in front of the trio, chittered at them, and scurried back into the woods. No doubt, the annoying furball was to blame for the trio's current dilemma.

Actius immediately gave up hope of getting the horse back because the beast ran too fast and had not been trained well enough to return. He had a passing thought that the horse would reach the town unaccompanied, resulting in a search party being dispatched, but he didn't want to rely on the idea. Actius picked up the broken restraints and looked at his companions, Roland and Finus. The two of them were still staring after the horse.

"Out in back and push now," he said.

The command was not given with any hint of anger, but it was short and to the point. Finus, being the youngest of the trio and the newest to the guild by more than five years, quickly obeyed. He seemed eager to please his master. Roland bit his lip and took his place next to Finus. He placed his hands on the rough wooden backend of the cart.

The cart had been designed with four wooden walls and a locking wooden side panel to protect the medicinal herbs inside. These plants were collected early in the spring and sold throughout the year by the guild. The structure of the cart caused it to be tall, lengthy, and heavy. The only saving grace was that it was late in the year and the guild was running low on stock. The unique cart design also allowed the guild to easily set up and close up shop in the various towns they visited. Often, they would stop on the road to sell to a fellow traveler before moving on. Much to Actius's current displeasure, the cart had not been built with a seat.

Finus and Roland began to push being careful of the large wheels which could have crushed their feet. Hour after hour as they pushed the cart, they were not overtaken by anyone on the road. This was both good and bad because they had no control over who would come upon them—a friend or a foe. Being alone on the road was not unusual and did little to upset Actius or Roland.

"Are there no travelers for the festivals? Does no one care about the spirits? About Halloween?" Finus asked Roland, looking over his shoulder at the still-deserted woodland behind them.

The trees cast long shadows across the road.

"Not by that name. It's All-Hallows, and people observe it in seclusion."

He said no more and Finus fell silent. Wind swept through the trees above them causing brown, yellow, orange, and purple leaves to flutter down to the cart.

Several more hours passed with Actius at the front of the cart and Roland and Finus at the rear. The sound from the wheels was continuous to the point that nobody noticed it anymore. They said no more to each other, using their strength for the task at hand. Luckily, they were all able-bodied individuals.

Actius pulled the restraints to steer the wagon around rocks and uneven surfaces on the road. In truth, he did little because the road was almost entirely straight. At the back of the cart, Roland thought Actius was to blame for the horse breaking free. Anger rose inside him with every few hundred feet they went. It had been Actius's choice to use a new horse to undertake the journey because he thought it would be faster than the reliable but slow mule they usually used in their travels. That mule was never spooked though.

Roland kept his thoughts to himself so he wouldn't have to argue. He simply hoped his companions wouldn't say anything to trigger an argument. He wanted to take over the guild one day and become the master himself, so he refused to take part in anything that would thwart his plans. With Actius getting older, it was only a matter of time before he stopped traveling altogether. One bad argument could mean the end of Roland's employment with the guild. It wasn't worth messing up.

Actius knew they had a while to go before they arrived at the town, but he hoped that without any breaks they would arrive before nightfall. He continued to watch the sun as it journeyed across the sky. Roland knew they were close as well, and he said as much to Finus as the sun began to set. The young man looked more worried than usual. That's when their day became worse and their limited luck ended without ceremony.

The wind picked up and the cart wobbled to the left and right. One of the wheels almost ran over Roland's foot. Then, Roland and Finus came to an abrupt stop. Finus actually walked into the cart. There was a loud crack. It sounded like a tree branch coming down. Something had happened up front. Finus rubbed his nose with the back of his hand and checked it for blood. There was none. The two of them walked around the side of the cart and saw Actius staring at the left-hand side of the now damaged front wheel. It wasn't bent, but it was lower than the rest of the cart. The bottom was stuck in a crack in the road.

The fissure was deep and there looked to be a large rock at one end of it.

The three merchants stared, unsure of what to do. Finus looked at Actius with pleading eyes. He did not want to camp in this part of the forest.

"Let's all try to lift it," said Actius with a low and gruff tone.

Finus stepped up to the wheel followed by Roland. It was difficult to fit next to each other but they managed. The three men grabbed the large wooden wheel and pulled as hard as they could but to no avail. The wheel didn't budge.

"What are we going to do?" asked Finus with an audible shake in his voice.

Actius stepped back and scratched his head. He made a low whistle. He looked up the road in both directions then back at the cart. He sniffed and wrinkled his nose.

"Roland, what do you think we should do?"

He asked the question without looking up.

Roland was surprised to be asked his opinion. For the past ten years, he had simply done as Actius instructed. He too looked at the setting sun. There was only about half an hour of light left.

"We should camp."

Finus let out an involuntary groan which was ignored. Actius nodded his head and walked to the back of the cart. Roland thought he saw the flash of a smile as he passed.

"Happy?" he asked Actius, more obnoxiously than he should have.

Actius looked over his shoulder and winked.

"Why, yes. Happy to camp out in the woods all night. Happy to follow your wise advice. Happy to not continue onward to the town. Happy. Happy. Happy."

Roland wasn't sure how to respond.

"We can't just abandon the cart," he eventually said. "What would we do in the morning if we came back to find it had been stolen in the night?"

Actius rummaged around the base of the wheels, grunting periodically. Finus looked uneasy at the side of the road.

"Of course. No sense in leaving the cart. You'll need it when you've got me out of the way," Actius mumbled. "Out of the way and out of your thoughts, no doubt."

Annoyed, Roland walked into the woods to search for some dry wood. They had been lucky enough to start a fire the night before because they had some wood on the cart, but he wasn't so sure that they would be able to find dry wood now. He was right, and he came back with some damp oak branches (the driest he could find), placing them near the cart.

A compartment slid out near the base of the cart. Actius produced a large bag and threw it to the side of the road. It contained the guild's camping equipment. Finus opened the bag and pulled out several furs, some bread, two rocks, and a jug of water.

Without the fire, the trio would be in for an extremely cold night. The sun set as Roland unsuccessfully tried to start the fire. He rotated a thick stick with a pointed end on one of the oak branches to try to produce a spark. A ferocious wind whipped through the camp as the trio clung to their furs. If it weren't for how loud the wind was, they could have heard their teeth chattering.

Roland continued to rotate the stick, but the fire refused to start. His hand cramped and he felt blisters forming on his palms. He stopped for a moment, glancing up to see Finus and Actius speaking to each other, but it was impossible to hear what they said over the wind. They hardly noticed that he had stopped trying to light the fire. He picked up the stick once more. This time, a spark ignited in the center of the branch and Roland gave a shout of surprise.

The sparks fluttered and fell on the other branches, extinguishing themselves. The wind had mercilessly caused the branch to go cold once more. Roland tried, again and again, focusing his attention on the stick and the tree branch. He ignored the pain and thought about the warmth he was trying to conjure. For how long after the sun set he tried to light the fire, he couldn't remember, but eventually he was tackled to the ground by a surprisingly strong Finus.

The leaves and dirt swirled around the two men as Roland tried to stand up and Finus continued to hold him to the ground. Actius was at the side, kicking Roland repeatedly in the stomach. With each blow, Roland became less aware of the pain he was experiencing and more aware of his surroundings. He had no time to consider his actions as he fought with his assailant.

"Why?" he sputtered.

Finus whispered in his ear, but he couldn't understand more than a few words: "Kill him..." "Split it evenly..."

Those short explanations resonated with Roland. Realizing this could be the end, he managed to push Finus off him, sending him rolling into a nearby depression in the dirt. He didn't try to attack Actius, instead, running deeper into the woods. Actius had been shouting something, but he caught none of it. The only thought on his mind was that of escape.

He ran and ran until he couldn't run anymore. His body had become extremely weak because of the intense physical exertion the day had demanded from him. The wind continued, but it no longer chilled his face and hands because he was so numb. His lungs burned and his stomach ached. He wanted to collapse to the ground and move no more.

He looked behind him but Actius and Finus were nowhere to be seen. This did little to ease his mind. He had no idea of which way to go, but he couldn't stay in the cold all night. His only hope was to find the nearby town. He chose a direction and walked, having been born with a fairly accurate internal sense of direction, he trusted in his instincts.

As the night wore on and the cold became almost too intense to bear, he began to shiver uncontrollably which made walking difficult. A rustle to his left. It wasn't the wind. He looked. The shadows in the woods played tricks on his mind. Trees stared back at him. They were tall with large, round trunks. He continued walking afraid if he stopped he would die. The hope he had for finding the town dwindled.

He bumped into something.

At first, he thought it was a tree. Then, that something moved and shrieked. It was a sound unlike the wind. A menacing sound tortured by the elements and amplified by the dense trees and foliage. Roland tried to back away but he was knocked to the ground. More pain in Roland's chest and limbs. The crushing and tearing of sinews snapping and skin tearing went on for several minutes. The figure of a dark horse haunted Roland's last moments.

The following morning, the runaway horse walked back up the road. Actius and Finus were surprised to see it. There were some dark stains on its hooves, but neither man paid them any mind. The duo managed to tame and attach the animal to the cart and the wheel came unstuck. Finus checked the cart for extensive damage and found none. They arrived in town an hour later and set up shop under a large oak tree in the center of the market district.

"Wasn't there three of you last year?" asked an old man with a milky white eye who had just bought several healing leaves.

Actius smiled.

Four

Light Under the Dark Cliff

You stand at the base of a steep, winding staircase carved into a seaside cliff. Far away, birds call to one another, but it's difficult to hear their individual cries. You taste salt in the air and you notice your tongue is dry. A slight breeze casts strands of hair in your face and sunlight warms your skin. You last blinked a long time ago.

You glance down and see you are wearing a white robe with a brown sash. You cannot see your feet but you know they are naked. The hard sandstone beneath you feels warm and gritty. For a moment, you are the space between your toes and the earth.

You feel stuck. Could you leave where you are? You don't feel like going and you don't know why. Does anyone know why? You realize you don't know how you got to the seacliff.

You look around you. An island with no land in sight. That is where you are.

Your eyes feel blue. What a strange thought. Your hair feels brown. Less strange. You think your hair is long and braided. Normal. You refuse to check to make sure. Why refuse?

The water to your left ripples and froths. It was quiet before. There are white clouds above you. They do not look puffy. They should look puffy.

The calm tranquility of your surroundings is interrupted by a loud, high-pitched noise. It might be the birds. A bright light comes from somewhere. Maybe it's coming from the void. You wonder if it's the sun. The sun is in the void. You stare into the light as everything around you dissolves into nothingness. What was around you? The light fluctuates, growing dimmer then brighter. Why would a light do that? The noise becomes one continuous tone. It goes on for so long you no longer hear it. The light no longer fluctuates. You stare into the light for so long it becomes darkness. It brightens until you see it again.

It stops.

You are once again standing at the base of the steps. What a beautiful place.

You raise your hand to your hair. It's braided. Why are you no longer refusing? You look around and see you are alone. Why did you not notice before?

You want to climb the steps so you try to move your feet forward. In your mind, you succeed. In reality, nothing happens. All you need to do is get your mind to produce reality. You try once more, summoning all of your energy into your right foot. Well, not all of it because that would be impossible. It moves nonetheless. You are not sure, but you think your body made a squeaking sound as your foot swung forward and landed on the first step. There are so many sounds you think you hear, it's difficult to tell which ones are important. Your feet take over. You are not moving them, but they move.

You climb the steps. This is how you walk. With each step, your feet feel dirtier and grittier. So filthy. The stones are smooth under the sand. The smoothness is less filthy. You do not know how many steps there are. Not that you are the one walking.

You can't see the top of the cliff from the angle you're at. If only you could try a different angle. But, you do see the cliff curves out of view instead of looming over you. In that way, the cliff is nice. You feel that the cliff cannot be tall. Not because tall people can't be nice but because that is how you feel.

You climb up switchbacks for ten minutes, getting farther and farther away from the sea. This is the first time you have hiked for this long without feeling a burning sensation in your calves and thighs. As you climb, you alternate between shadowed areas covered by the cliff and light areas infiltrated by the sun.

You think of nothing. As soon as a thought forms, it disappears as though it never existed. You are only aware of your surroundings. They are beautiful.

Before you know it--before you can know it-- you reach the top of the cliff. You were right; it was not tall. There are no more steps to climb. A part of you dies at the thought of reaching the top. In this space, there is no stone, only dirt. It's dark brown. The same color you would expect wet dirt to be, but it does not feel wet. There are also several pine trees at the top of the cliff. They, of course, are green. The trees are near several boulders and a few bushes. The bushes are, not so of course, black. Not a deep purple. Just, black.

You walk toward the trees. You hear the tree wind which sounds different from the sea wind. You notice the sky is no longer blue. Strange how things change so quickly. It has become a dark brown. Not as dark as the dirt, though. There are hints of gray along the horizon. Gray is such a colorless color, you think. Then, that thought goes away.

The entire sky is filled with lightning and thunder. The strands of lightning are white. If the sky was a different color, the lightning would have been yellow. The earth beneath you, however, is not affected by the changing sky. It glows as if it were still under the blue sky.

You look directly above you and you see where the sun should be, but there is no sun. The void has hidden it. There is only a bright spot. The hint of sun.

You look back down at the dirt and you notice a park bench. You approach it, unsure of what to do. You feel like you should sit. The feeling comes from inside you, or, perhaps, not inside you. You are unsure. You are unsure of whether you are unsure. You feel like you have facial features which could make a perplexed look but you are unsure of whether you have facial features. Your eyes still feel blue. That is important. It's important to you.

There is a pressure in your chest--the first feeling you've had since arriving at the cliff. True feeling. Pain. Not a sense--a feeling. Before you understand the pain, it leaves.

You no longer feel anything.

You approach the bench and sit down. What a sturdy bench.

When you sit, you notice the bench is occupied. You turn and look. It's not a person. It's a lengthy figure of darkness. The darkness comes from the cloud of smoke which has engulfed the figure. You are unsure of whether the figure is not actually made up of smoke. There is no face, but there is a place for a face. You are unsure of whether the limbs you see are arms or legs but you know the figure has both.

You're not frightened.

You know you should be frightened.

You're not frightened.

You stare across the sea. It has become tumultuous. The lightning continues. There is thunder, although the thunder is silent. You know there is thunder because you can feel it.

The sky deepens in its brownness. It's odd it doesn't simply turn black. You look down at the waves crashing on the cliffside beneath you. Under the water, there is a bright light. It calls to you. You do not know what it says. It is not a language you know. The sounds are low and high.

Do you know what a whale sounds like? Have you ever seen a whale?

The sounds continue.

The dark figure next to you moves slightly and you're unsure of why it moved. You look back at the sea and notice the light has become brighter underneath the waves. You now understand what the light says, but you are unsure of the meaning. It's words. You have forgotten what words mean. You have forgotten everything.

You are...

There is no longer a dark figure next to you. It glides away. It has no need for legs. If you could think, you would think to follow it.

You look back at the sea which is now a raging hurricane. The lightning dances atop the circular shape. You are unsure of how you are able to see an entire hurricane from a park bench atop a seacliff. That is a thought though, so you accept what you see to avoid thinking.

The cliffside crumbles and you fall.

You fall into the wet sea.

But you are not drowning.

You are not afraid.

Light engulfs you.

Darkness above you.

Light engulfs you.

Darkness...

Etched in stone, words for the dead:
"I scattered your ashes on the cliffside.
October 31, 1942 - October 31, 1973"
The good they do is not for them.

Five

Duffel Bags and Dragons

I PACKED MY DUFFEL bag with rocks, gold dollars, and a plastic sword. Then, I sat down on the edge of my bed and waited.

Two long hours passed while I read comics, organized my action figures, and stared at the ceiling. "This is so boring," I continually muttered to myself. At length, the alarm clock on my nightstand read 11:42 p.m. That was when I heard it—PA-TWINK—the signal!

"Finally," I said, flinging my blanket into a corner where it landed on a stack of heavily-worn chapter books. I slid open my second-story window and a dry July breeze drifted into my room.

Bill, my best friend, stared back at me from his room. He wore a big goofy grin and held an airsoft gun in his right hand.

Our houses were identical: tan, tall, and skinny, with about four feet of grass separating them. Why the builder decided to place the houses so close together, I'll never know.

The rest of our neighbors were up on the mountainside but their homes weren't visible through the trees. Our community was small; and, according to my mom, that was supposedly a good thing.

"Ahoy there, matey," Bill said to me in his best pirate voice. I smiled and thought about earlier in the day.

All afternoon, we had played pirates in the park behind our houses. When Bill went home for dinner, we had agreed to resume playing after his parents went to bed.

Now, his eyepatch was back on and a plastic sword hung from his belt.

"Shiver me timbers," I said.

I put my own eyepatch on and looked for my sword but remembered that I had put it in the black duffel bag with the rest of my toys. I lifted this from off my desk.

"Get the rope, captain," I said. My pirate voice wasn't as good as Bill's.

I placed the duffel bag onto the dresser beneath my window. Bill bent over and picked up a thick piece of rope with a loop at each end. He tossed one loop to me and I pulled it through the window and put it over my bedpost. Once I was done, Bill did the same thing with the rope in his room, and it went taut. This was our bridge.

I undid the duffel bag handle and looped it around the rope (like so many times before), tied it, and pushed it out so that Bill could pull it into his room. That was where our pirate fort was located.

I decided that I had better cross over into Bill's room once he grabbed the duffel bag before he had to tell me to because Bill always said pirates were brave.

The bag dangled on the rope between our two houses and Bill reached out to grab it—SNAP—the handle failed.

I watched the bag fall, but it didn't reach the ground uninterrupted: THUD. I tore off my eyepatch to get a better look.

"It hit something," Bill said. I barely heard him because, even in the dark, I saw that "something" was a someone. The boy in question was sprawled out on the ground next to the duffel bag, just lying in the grass.

Bill gasped, and I knew that he had seen the boy too. I immediately thought of getting my mom but I stopped, afraid of being punished. I justified to myself that this wasn't my fault.

"How could you?" I asked, looking up at Bill. He was still staring down with his mouth open, but his head jerked up, and our eyes met. Well, my eyes, his eye; he was still wearing his eyepatch.

"Me? It's your duffel bag," he replied, drawing his plastic sword from his belt loop and pointing it at me. His airsoft gun had disappeared inside his room somewhere.

"You let it drop. And, put your sword down."

"It was an accident."

A small coupe sped down the street in front of our houses. Hardly any cars ever came this way late at night, so it was most likely a neighbor. I felt sweaty and sick thinking about getting caught.

Bill lowered his sword, took off his eyepatch, and entered what I always referred to as Leadership Mode. This was when his face would harden and his eyes would bulge out from under his raised eyebrows. Usually, Bill reserved this attitude for when we played soldiers in the woods, but we weren't playing now.

"Asher, we need to help him. You coming?"

I didn't answer because I'm not a leader like Bill. I wanted to crawl under my covers and forget about what had happened. He saw my helpless expression and didn't like it.

"Come on, sissy. Just, go down to the yard. I'll do all of the important stuff."

I couldn't believe it. He called that strip of grass a yard, but it was an alleyway of death, and I didn't want to go. Bill looked persistent, though, and we needed to get the duffel bag.

I didn't trust myself to speak so I simply nodded and walked downstairs quietly. My mom's room was on the other side of the top floor, so I didn't worry about waking her when I closed the front door behind me.

Bill beat me to the disaster zone. He was leaning over the boy with a flashlight and a small first-aid kit when I arrived. I noticed that the boy's clothes were wet.

"He looks a little younger than us," Bill said as I approached. He looked up when I didn't respond. "Oh, don't look like that, he's only unconscious." Only unconscious? He said it as though it was the greatest news in the world.

I looked more closely at the boy. He had bleach-blond hair and a skinny frame, sort of like me. I leaned down and listened to his breathing. "Why are his clothes wet?" I asked.

Bill pointed straight down the alleyway to the park's pond behind our houses. Just then, I heard a groan, and I took a step back.

The boy was moving and his eyes were open. He sat up and looked at us for half a second before leaping up and running back toward the pond. He ran in vain though because Bill caught up to him and grabbed his suspenders before he had reached the end of the alleyway.

The boy struggled for a moment. "Red, Red!" he called. I worried for a moment about my mom hearing him, but to my relief, he stopped yelling.

"Don't hurt me," he said, holding his hands across his chest. His big hazel eyes were wet with tears.

"Hey, who do I look like, the Boogieman?" Bill let go of the confused boy and ushered him over to a nearby park bench in front of the pond.

I came over and sat down next to them. I noticed that the boy looked how I felt: scared. Part of me was relieved that he wasn't dead or stuck in a coma for years.

"What's your name?" I asked.

"Kobar," he said warily. I looked over at Bill for help, but he only shook his head as if to say, "Don't push it," so we sat in silence until Kobar started talking again.

"Have you seen a small, red dragon?" he asked.

"A dragon?" we blurted out in unison. Bill looked surprised and excited. I probably just looked surprised because dragons don't exist; and, if they did, they would be scary.

I had read books about dragons and seen movies where people died horrible deaths in their fiery dragon breath. It was one thing to play dragons, it was another to see a real one.

"What does this dragon look like?" asked Bill. He leaned in closer to Kobar, and I admit that I too inched closer to our new-found companion. He was growing on me quickly even if I didn't believe his developing story.

Kobar looked less frightened now. "I'll tell you if you promise to help me find him."

I looked over at Bill unsure, but he answered, "We promise."

"I met Red about a week ago when I went out to milk the cows. We started talking—"

"Talking to a dragon? He didn't eat you?" I said sarcastically. Bill punched my shoulder.

"Let him talk!"

Kobar gave me a puzzled look and began his story again while I rubbed my stinging bruise. "Dragons don't eat people. At least, not where I'm from. I guess it's not the same here.

"Anyway, I liked him from the start because he is a runt like me... picked on by the other bigger dragons. I mean, I'm picked on by my brothers, but it was basically the same. So, he met me every day out by the barn where all of the cows are. We have a lot of cows too, for feeding dragons, you know."

"You feed dragons?" I asked. Bill punched me again. "Sorry. Go on."

"Of course we feed them. How else would we pay them for rides? So like I was—"

"You ride the—" I stopped short as Bill moved his arm. "Sorry. Continue."

"Well, you see, that's where the problem started. Of course, you know that children aren't allowed to ride dragons. At least, not where I'm from, maybe things are different here," he added, making a sweeping motion with his hand.

"But today, I convinced Red that we should go riding to see what it's like. See, nobody rides Red because he is too small to go fast. He didn't like the idea at first because he was afraid someone would see us. If that happened, my family would get fined by the town and Red would be banished by the larger dragons, or worse...

"I've been whipped before for stuff, like doing chores too slow or staying out later than usual, but now I've really done it. My mother... She'll whip me until I'm all crippled if she finds out. I have to get back soon."

Kobar looked down at his lap and started to cry. "Oh, Red, I'm sorry. Where are you?" We waited for him to come back to reality. Bill patted him on the back and I tried not to breathe too loud. I knew that whenever I was upset little things like loud breathing would annoy me.

Kobar sighed and sat up straight. He was looking at the pond.

"We went flying after I finished milking the cows. I climbed up on his back—it was rough and dull, kind of leathery, but extremely warm. I was surprisingly comfortable sitting between his back and neck spines. Then, we took off. I loved the feeling of being free from the ground, up in the cool air with the sun's rays warming my back.

"Well, we went out across the forest, and right as we passed over the lake area I started to feel dizzy. I remember falling through the air. It felt the same way as when I fall in a dream before waking up, but I couldn't wake up. I remember something cold... I think I fell into a lake. Red must have been chasing after me, and the next thing I remember is waking up on the side of this pond and walking off for help."

"And then you had to hit him with your duffel bag," said Bill. He grinned at me and I punched him. "I know this sounds crazy, Kobar, but I think I know what happened. It's just like that sci-fi movie I saw last week with the wormhole." Ben stood up and walked in front of us, ready to enlighten us about his theory.

"Two spaceships were warping through space when they went through a wormhole and even though they were right next to each other, time screwed up and the first spaceship had to wait forever for the next one to arrive."

"This isn't Star Trek, Spock," I said sarcastically.

Bill glared at me. Kobar looked confused.

"I don't think we have to wait twenty years because a wormhole in space is like billions of times bigger than this pond." Bill was rambling now. "I'm pretty sure there is a connection between size and time. So, hopefully, Red will be coming through our pond-portal any time now. That is, assuming he dove in after you, Kobar."

Kobar looked hopefully up at Bill. "Really?"

The timing couldn't have been better because just as Kobar asked his question, I saw a bright white speck appear at the bottom of the pond. It got bigger, and the bigger it got the faster it grew until the whole pond was a shining beacon of light.

Something shot out of the pond, splashing water on all three of us. I saw a silhouette in the sky, then I was up in the air. The thing had grabbed me! The world swayed around and I saw blurs of Bill somewhere near me. Kobar was calling out from down below: "Stop! Stop!"

At this point, everything went black and I was barely conscious of the grass once more beneath my back. It felt so good, even in my groggy state of mind. I blinked several times before my vision returned to me, and I saw Bill lying next to me.

I sat up and saw Red, in all his glory. The water was shimmering on his scales, and he didn't look like a runt, he looked like a magnificent dragon to me. Bill gasped and I knew that he was staring too. I really couldn't believe it.

"I told you! What did I tell you? Wormholes." Ben got up and started dancing like a fool. His arms flailed all around him as he turned in circles while shaking his legs.

I was sure that the commotion would have woken everybody in the neighborhood but to my surprise, nobody was coming down the mountain, and our houses remained still and silent.

Kobar was standing next to Red explaining what had happened. The dragon nodded its large head.

Red spoke for the first time and his voice was low and gravelly. "I'm sorry for attacking. I saw Kobar with you and I thought he was shackled to this hostage contraption, and that you two were the guards." Red tapped the bench with his wing.

My body was shaking and I felt woozy, but I was smiling, almost laughing. I couldn't believe that I was meeting a real dragon. Bill collapsed on the ground, laughing hysterically. He was muttering something about hostages and contraptions. Kobar jumped up on Red's back.

"Well, my mom is going to kill me if we don't get back. Bill, do you think this portal works the other way too?"

Bill stopped laughing and wiped a finger under his eye. "Yeah, it should. Just fly above it and dive in. And, promise you'll visit us soon? Like, tomorrow night?"

Kobar was beaming. "You bet."

I nodded at Kobar when he looked at me, and he smiled back.

"Thank you for helping us," Red said. The low vibrations from his voice traveled up and down my spine. It reminded me of when Bill would practice his electric guitar.

Red flapped his massive wings, and I wondered what a big dragon looked like. He flew up above the pond into the moonless sky, a black shadow against the starless universe. Red dove headfirst, Kobar hanging on with all of his might, into the pond.

A bright light followed and water splashed us again. I looked over at Bill whose expression was somewhere between gaping and smiling.

"That was awesome!" he screamed, flinging his hands into the air. "Thanks for hitting him with your duffel bag." Just as quickly as his excitement came, his face changed to be more thoughtful. "Hmmm, I wonder..."

"Hey!" I exclaimed. "My duffel bag." I turned around and ran back to get it. The bag was still lying on the ground in the alleyway. I reached down and undid the zipper. Everything was still safe including our prized rocks. I zipped it back up and realized that Bill was not next to me. I looked back out of the alleyway toward the pond.

"Bill?" I asked.

My only greeting was the sound of water splashing, followed by a bright flash. I ran to the edge of the pond and looked at the light fading away in the distance.

"Really, Bill? Without me?" I looked around. "How did you travel through?" I saw a long straight piece of PVC pipe lying next to the pond. I picked it up, knowing exactly what to do.

I backed up about twenty feet, holding the pipe like a pole-vaulter, then I ran straight for the pond. I put the end of the pipe down into the ground and my body launched into the air. For a moment, I hovered, about ten feet above the water, then I fell: SPLASH.

Six

The Whiskey Crate

"YOUR HEAD'S GOING TO get blown clean off your neck, Randy. Don't get me wrong, I support you, but he'll kill you," said Tom as he saddled a horse and led it to the stable's back gate.

The sheriff followed on his own horse in the swaying lantern's light, which cast yellowish hues into the darkness. In the sky, a full moon shifted between clouds, like a pebble swimming through a current.

"Doesn't matter, Tom. I'm the sheriff. I've got a duty to the town."

Tom snorted. "You mean you have a duty to Elizabeth. Don't try and pretend you're doing this for the town."

Randy smiled. "All right, I love her. You know that, but I love the town too."

"Love the town? You haven't even been here two weeks. No. You're crazy about a girl." Tom led the horse around a hole in the dirt. "I know her family situation isn't right, but what happens if you're caught? Her father will make all of us pay."

Randy shook his head. "The mayor's a tyrant. I tried talking to him. I took him aside at the party, but he's always drunk. After the dance, he left with his arm so firm around Elizabeth, she winced. I know he's doing more to her than that when they're no people around."

"She's a pretty girl, but—"

"Stop it right there." Randy pulled up on his horse's reins until it stopped. "I'm going to save Elizabeth and her mom, Mary. She doesn't love her husband any more than you do." Tom opened his mouth, but Randy cut him off again. "He's chained together five padlocks on the outside of his cellar door to hold. Do you want to guess what's on the other side?"

Tom let his mouth hang open for a second and closed it again. A moment later, he said, "You're right. I'll come if you want."

Randy shook his head. "Thanks, but I just need your horse for the getaway. I don't need you in any more danger than you already are."

Tom nodded his head and stared across the half-harvested wheat field. A split-handled scythe lay propped against some hay bales and the smell of fresh manure wafted from the stable. A distant plow looked like a lean cow in the moonlight. The field ended near the mountain's base just before the mayor's house, which sat in solitude, almost hidden behind the trees.

Tom shuffled his feet. "Are you going to kill him?"

Randy didn't hesitate a second. "Sure, I'll kill him. No father should treat his family like a pack of wild dogs."

Tom nodded his head. "True."

"Do you think anyone will be mad if we get a new mayor? Of course not. Everybody hates him." Randy sighed. "Listen, thanks for your help."

Tom nodded his head again. "Just bring Martha back. Don't let that bag explode on her." He gestured to the pack on Martha's side and stroked Martha's neck before handing the reins to Randy.

"I'll keep the horses safe." Randy tapped his spurs into his horse's sides, and both horses broke into a trot, leaving Tom to gaze after them.

A few minutes later, Randy saw the mayor's house become more visible through the elm and willow trees. He heard the small mountain stream running past the old wood structure. He had the horses stop at the field's edge. Martha stood statue-still next to him.

Carefully, Randy unbuckled Martha's saddlebag and pulled back the leather top, revealing several sticks of dynamite. A long brown fuse coiled out of the top of the bag.

Randy checked to make sure the fuse was connected to all of the sticks, then he surveyed the land, deciding how best to proceed. The mayor owned a lot of land, which consisted mostly of brown dirt. A few patches of grass dotted the stream bank, and some boulders helped break up the open space.

The stream ran toward the house before cutting through the front yard, so Randy proceeded along the water's edge as far as he could. Near the house, the horses waded through the stream with Randy guiding them. A cold breeze came down the mountain, and on the far side of the stream, branches cracked, leaves rustled and Martha fell into a pit, shrieking violently. Wooden stakes impaled her body, and she never made another sound.

Inside the house, Elizabeth's eyes sprang open; her heart hammered. Paralyzed, she listened to a heart-wrenching wail coming from outside. Her mother, Mary, was standing next to the cellar door, peering through a slit in the wood. A candle dimly lit the room.

"What's that? Is it Randy?" Elizabeth asked. Her hopes and fears surfaced. She had been expecting him to try something for several days now. She ran over to the door.

At first, she didn't notice anyone, but then she spotted a man on horseback twenty yards away. If it hadn't been for the moonlight, she wouldn't have seen anything.

"Randy!" she exclaimed.

"Get away from the door," said a voice from behind her.

"Ran—" Elizabeth shouted, but her father, Mayor the mayor, cut her off.

"Shut up!" He walked—mostly stumbled—down the cellar stairs. He walked over to Elizabeth, swaying back and forth as he did so, and grabbed her by the shoulders. His sweat and breath reeked, causing Elizabeth to turn her head.

"You think you're safe? Nobody's saving you tonight." He clasped Elizabeth to his chest.

"Let me go!"

"I just want a hug." The squeezing intensified for a moment and then he shoved her back. He raised his unbalanced fist, steadied it, and punched Elizabeth in the face.

"Don't hit her," Mary whispered from the corner. The mayor looked over at her; his eyes blazed.

"I'll do whatever I want, Mary. In fact..." the mayor swung his fist in a large arc, striking Elizabeth's face again.

"Stop!" Mary shrieked.

He shoved Elizabeth to the ground and took a step toward Mary.

"Oh, save us, Randy," whispered Elizabeth.

The mayor stopped, his eyes bulged, and his body went rigid. "I already told you, nobody is saving you." He grasped Elizabeth's hair, yanked her to her feet, and shoved her again. Her head hit the brick wall with a crack. The mayor was breathing deeply now. He paced back and forth, swaying from side to side. Sweat gleamed on his skin. "That dumb boy. If it weren't for him... Look what he's made me do."

Elizabeth was barely conscious on the ground. "Tell Randy I love him," she said.

"Shut it! I'm the only man you need," said the mayor. He stopped pacing and turned toward his wife. "Don't look at me that way, Mary."

The mayor approached Mary, always stepping too far to the right or left, like a newborn calf. He jabbed her stomach, kept her standing, and jabbed again. Elizabeth struggled breathing and tears slipped from her eyes.

"Stop crying!" the mayor hollered. He dropped Mary and staggered back up the stairs. Half-conscious, Elizabeth heard the stairs groan, and the door into the house slam. She crawled into her mother's arms and listened to the chilling crack of a rifle.

Randy's ears rang and his heart hammered; Martha's corpse eyed the sheriff from the bottom of the pit. He carefully maneuvered his own horse around more leaves and sticks. Minutes passed, and the house remained still and dark, but that did little to ease Randy's mind. "Sorry, Martha. I let you down," he whispered.

He waited for a few minutes, making sure the house stayed silent, then slid his foot from the stirrup, wanting to retrieve the explosives from Martha's saddlebag, when a loud crack filled the night air, and a bullet grazed his arm. He flicked the reins, and his horse took off. Another bullet ricocheted off the gray surface of a nearby rock.

Randy drew his pistol from his holster. He rode quickly, firing at the house to scare the mayor. A few seconds later, he had successfully backtracked to the pit. He grabbed the lip of the pit and lowered himself, keeping his legs bent away from the stakes. Holding himself up with one arm, he reached toward Martha's saddlebag. He heard another gunshot and his horse fell. Randy clenched his teeth and closed his eyes.

"I'm gonna kill him," he said.

He grabbed the explosives and placed them on the ground. He pulled himself up, just high enough to see over his dying horse. The mayor was aiming through the front window next to the door. The drunk man shot again and Randy ducked; the bullet sank deep into the horse, which finally stopped breathing.

Randy crawled out of the hole and lay behind his horse. The rifle shot again, and he bolted toward the cellar, keeping the explosives tucked under his arm. The mayor shot once more, but the bullet ricocheted off a tree trunk.

"Randy?" Elizabeth asked as he approached.

"Elizabeth stay back. I'm gonna blow the door."

"What? Ran—"

"Quickly! Get back before I light the fuse."

Elizabeth and her mother ducked behind a thin mattress on the cellar's far side. The initial trauma of their beating had subsided.

Randy placed the explosives at the base of the door and he held his revolver above the fuse. His hand held steady, he pulled the trigger, and a spark from the gun ignited the fuse. The front door crashed open at the same time.

"Where are ya?" bellowed the mayor.

Randy turned around, accidentally dropped his pistol, and started running. Not thinking, he went in the direction of his horse. Dirt flew, and the world rushed around him. The mayor pulled his trigger. Randy collapsed, holding his side, while blood trickled between his fingers.

The mayor stood in front of the house hollering at the moon when the explosives went off. Startled, and somewhat deaf, he turned around and saw smoldering debris strewn across his property. Small flames illuminated the new smoke. The mayor turned back around and raised his rifle. Randy scooted a few feet away, and another bullet grazed his shoulder.

Elizabeth stepped out of the cellar, saw Randy on the ground, and gasped. Her mother followed her out of the cellar, coughing.

"Randy!" Elizabeth shouted. She ran to him, knelt beside him, and grabbed his blood-covered hand.

"Run," said Randy. His voice sounded hollow.

"I gotta stop the bleeding. Stop talking." Elizabeth tore a long strip from her dress.

"He's coming."

"Stop! You're going to hurt yourself." Elizabeth wrapped the fabric around Randy's side.

"Go!"

The mayor staggered in a line, swearing and waving his gun. Mary had disappeared in the smoke.

"I don't know if I'll ever get the chance again," said Elizabeth. Her lips pressed against Randy's. A warmth sprang up between the two of them. For a moment, they weren't in peril. Then, the mayor kicked Elizabeth in the side and aimed his rifle at Randy.

"This is my town! This is my family!"

A gunshot rang out and Elizabeth screamed. The mayor fell to the earth. Mary, now a widow, stood behind him holding Randy's revolver. "You ain't my family!" She looked ghastly.

Elizabeth looked at Mary with wide eyes. "Mama," she barely breathed.

Mary didn't answer right away. The gun's smoke covered her face and made her eyes water. "He can't hurt you."

The sound of horse hooves could be heard in the distance. Some men from town rode into the firelight. Tom led the group and dismounted next to Randy. "What happened?" Tom caught his breath. "You've been shot? Doctor!"

"Martha fell," said Randy. Tom ignored him. A man with a lengthy white beard rushed over to Randy. Elizabeth placed Randy's head in her hands while the man examined Randy's wound.

At the same time, two middle-aged men talked to Mary. They nodded their heads and one placed a hand on her shoulder. "Throw him in the fire," she said. "Right on a whiskey crate! He'd have wanted a funeral with alcohol."

The men grabbed the mayor and carried him to the burning house. Nobody cared that they smiled.

Tom watched the rest of the men go to the pit where Randy's horse lay dead. "Looks like you lost your horse too, sheriff. I think that's enough death for one day."

Seven

Mr. Watts' Money

THE MONEY WAS MISSING. That is if it had been there in the first place. But, Mr. Watts was too shocked by the overall lack of cash to realize this point right away. He was in the midst of assuming that it had been stolen.

The money—$5000—was supposed to be in the unlikely spot of a red biohazard receptacle at the back of a biology classroom supply closet. Mr. Watts, of course, was the resident biology teacher, and this was his supply closet. It was a drop zone, pure and simple.

For whatever reason, the receptacle remained empty except for a florescent-orange, heavy-duty trash bag which lined the inside. The lid was propped up by the foot lever which Mr. Watts was holding down with the point of his right wing-tipped shoe.

Yellow, untainted sunlight streamed in through a surprisingly clean single-paned window near the top of the closet. Five shelves ran along the supply closet walls; all of them were covered with broken microscopes, chipped beakers, ratty tarps, and lidless mason jars. A couple of mouse traps lay on the floor, surrounded by droppings, ironically cleaned of their cheese.

Through the open supply closet door, Mr. Watts looked like a mannequin—perhaps broken—resting alongside the old equipment. His shoulders were slumped, his head was lowered, and his blue dress shirt was wrinkled. He was like a statue. In fact, he hadn't moved for at least five minutes. Luckily, the classroom was empty, so nobody could call the situation what it was: odd.

Mr. Watts knew deep down that he was staring into an empty receptacle, but he couldn't bring himself to let himself know what he already knew... the money wasn't there. Sweat beaded on the old man's forehead magnifying his wrinkles and sliding down into his sideburns. His face was whiter than it should have been, and he was leaning against one of the shelves.

He breathed because he had to, but it was shallow and he felt dizzy. The stream of sunlight moved slowly up his frail body as the sun lowered in the sky. When it reached his eyes, he blinked. With that blink, he allowed himself to finally know that the money wasn't there.

The lid clanged shut and Mr. Watts shuffled into his classroom. He smoothed strands of gray hair from his eyes and licked his chapped lips while he searched the top of his desk for a white calendar. He found it and pulled it from under a stack of ungraded tests next to an empty blue tissue box. It was flipped open to March.

A few handwritten names were scrawled on every calendar day including today. These names represented absent students, but the name Mr. Watts so desperately wanted to find on this second Friday in March didn't appear on the list: Kyle Crofts. This could only mean one thing, Mr. Watts thought, that Kyle had been to class and hadn't left the agreed-upon money in the supply closet.

Mr. Watts flipped back to October and found a black "X" scratched across the second Friday's box. He turned to November and saw the same "X" marked on the second Friday. December, January, and February all followed this pattern, but March was still blank.

The teacher eyed the black and gold fountain pen on his desk. He wanted to grab that pen, push the top down until it clicked, and draw two diagonal lines in a crisscross pattern over today, but he couldn't because the money wasn't there. Instead, his weedy, white eyebrows contorted into a furry snake as he decided on what to do next.

The school library was the logical place to go in order to find Kyle without rousing suspicion. Calling him on the phone would leave a record of communication for the police to pick up on later... if they ever found out. Heading to the student's dorms in the west wing would be sure to start gossip as Mr. Watts had never been there before. The library; then, was the best place for Mr. Watts to go, so he went with a sweaty handkerchief in his pocket and a forced smile on his face.

When he arrived, he picked a random book entitled Historical Trivia from off a tan cart and sat at a lone corner desk on the second-floor balcony which afforded him a perfect view of the library's entrance.

Several groups of students studied quietly on the main floor while a few loners with heavy backpacks browsed the shelves. The sun was setting on the outside world, but it seemed as though time didn't exist in the library as the ceiling lights simply turned on.

Twenty minutes after the lights came on, Kyle walked into the library, and much to Mr. Watts' delight, he was by himself. The teacher watched Kyle trip over a taped-down extension cord.

The professor thought of how to approach Kyle without anyone seeing. He immediately dismissed waving Kyle over because there was a good chance that he would simply bolt upon seeing his debt-collecting biology teacher.

The only thing Mr. Watts could do was watch and wait until Kyle was in a place far away from everyone else.

A few minutes went by. Mr. Watts saw his opportunity. He descended to a narrow walkway between two bookshelves where Kyle stood staring at the bottom shelf. Mr. Watts walked up beside his victim.

"Looking for something?" he whispered.

Kyle sucked in a sharp breath. "Mr. Watts!" he exclaimed turning on the spot.

"Yes?" asked Mr. Watts with an authoritative tone. He was beside himself with glee over having surprised Kyle. In fact, he wasn't even mad about the noisy response.

"What are you doing here?" asked Kyle. A few beads of sweat were visible on his brow.

"I'm looking for something," replied Mr. Watts. He clasped his hands in front of him.

Kyle's face turned green. "What're you looking for?"

Mr. Watts hated being asked questions he thought were stupid. "You know very well what. But, if I must spell it out for you..." He sighed. "The biohazard receptacle is empty."

Kyle's eyes darted from the bookshelf to Mr. Watts' face as though he were deciding whether or not he knew what Mr. Watts was talking about. He opened his mouth and closed it, twice. His legs shook and his hair matted to his forehead. He opened his mouth a third time.

"I know," was his reply. His voice was raspy, "Don't be mad, though. You can't be mad. I don't want you mad. If I had known you were going to be mad, I mean, I knew you were going to be mad—"

"Stop saying 'mad'," demanded Mr. Watts.

"Oh, okay. Yeah, I mean, I knew you would be angry. But, I don't... Well, now, I don't have the money." Kyle dropped his gaze before whispering, "Don't be mad."

"What do you mean you don't have it? Your parents are filthy rich," hissed the teacher. "You attend the best school in the region."

"I know," mouthed the terrified student.

"Do you? Because I don't think you do. You had it before. What happened?" Mr. Watts had hardly moved, but his knuckles were now white.

Kyle gulped. "I'm broke. I've always been broke. All the money I've ever given you wasn't mine."

Mr. Watts took a step back. This was not what he had expected to hear. "Who gave it to you?" he asked.

"Nobody gave it to me. I had to steal it." His voice was shaking.

Mr. Watts placed his hands on his head. His gray hair fell into his face and dark sweat swiveled between his shirt collar and pulsing neck. His vision clouded until all he could see was Kyle's pale face. "Where did you steal it from?"

"I've... I've been skimming it from the student body fund," Kyle explained, afraid his blackmailing teacher might become a murdering teacher at any moment. "I'm treasurer, or I was treasurer, and Dean Herbert gave me control of the account so I could gain some experience. And everything was going great up until this morning when he found out."

Mr. Watts dropped his arms and leaned into the bookshelf. "How did he find out?"

"He usually takes a morning walk, which is when I take the money. However, he skipped his walk this morning and walked in on me taking it from the safe. But, don't be mad, Mr. Watts. I didn't tell him why I was taking it. I mean, I did, but I lied and told him my family had medical bills. Well, that's not a lie, but I wasn't stealing for any medical bills."

Mr. Watts couldn't believe what he was hearing. "And he won't punish you?"

Kyle looked thoughtful for a moment. "No. He hasn't really said, but I don't think he will. Obviously, I'm not treasurer anymore, though."

Mr. Watts pursed his lips. "Why didn't you tell me this earlier?"

"What for?" asked Kyle. "You're just going to tell everyone my transcripts are fake."

Mr. Watts laughed and rested his head against some hardcover books. "You're right, I would have. But, I can't now, can I?"

Kyle shifted uncomfortably where he stood. "What do you mean?"

"What do I mean?" mocked Mr. Watts. "I mean our arrangement is at an end. No more money drops and no more blackmail. In fact, don't ever talk to me again."

Kyle's face lit up. "I promise I never will."

The two parted. Mr. Watts went back to his classroom, and Kyle studied in the library.

In July of that year, Mr. Watts took a month-long snorkeling trip to Fiji despite his small teaching salary; and, the following school year, he became involved in school government. His self-appointed duty was to oversee the new treasurer.

Eight

This Past Hour

DON'T—JUST DON'T. PLEASE. IT'S cold.

Night fell, the moon rose, and seventy-eight candles burned brightly. They were located in the neatly furnished master bedroom of a ranch-style home in southern Oregon. Ten tall white ones dripped on the black headboard. Other squatty ones with pools of wax rested together on two black nightstands. An old married couple occupied the room. The wife was alive; the husband had been dead for a week.

For one week, Edna Hatch hadn't noticed death's foul odor, nor had she seen the changes to her Ernest's bloated, pale body. She worried religiously, not that the neighbors would find her, but that she wouldn't be able to bring the man she had killed with a salmon back to life. He had choked. She had watched.

I don't care. Not now.

The wood clock in the corner chimed twelve times. Edna's wrinkled face sagged in the dancing shadows of the flickering candlelight. The scars on her forearms looked fresh. She cut the tip of her finger with a gleaming silver knife and watched the blood stream into her cupped hand. The sting felt good, but the blood felt better. "Sil vor con ni ni con vor sil," she chanted over and over again. She read from a printed sheet of paper at the foot of the bed.

The simple verse released powerful energy into the room. The darkness deepened, and the flames grew hotter. Edna stretched her arm and bent her palm. Blood splattered her husband's suit, the chanting continued. The blood dried on Edna's hand and the last drop fell. She stopped chanting, her throat paralyzed. Her eyes closed. She heard the window bang open and the wind howled into the room for a moment, then the window shut. She opened her eyes. The candles were out.

Do you remember? Please, try.

Edna flipped on the lights and gasped. The body had vanished. An imprint was left. The air seemed cleaner than before despite the smoke. Edna furrowed her brow. "Did it work?" she whispered. The night suddenly seemed like a dream.

Someone knocked on the bedroom door. Edna turned. This wasn't part of the plan. She gripped the knife tightly and raised the blade to her neck. Her backup plan seemed to be becoming a reality. The door was locked. "Is someone there?" she asked, wondering if there really had been a knock.

Not this time. I've chosen.

The knock came again. The knife slipped and a line of blood seeped from the cut. Edna winced. She looked at the wet blade and touched the wound. The blood was warm, but the wound was shallow. She held her hand over it and said, "Answer me. Who is there?" Her voice shook. There was no answer. Edna felt she knew who might be there. She looked at the brass doorknob and raised the knife back to her throat. "I'll do it! I've got a knife."

Edna uncovered her cut and grabbed the doorknob. She rotated the lock in the center. Fresh blood trickled down her neck with every heartbeat. The knife wobbled. Time passed. Edna slid the knife across her neck in her thoughts repeatedly. She wanted to do it; it would be easier than opening the door. Then again, hadn't this been her purpose all along? She knew who had knocked. It had to be him. The blade pushed deeper. What was she afraid of?

Dying—like this—isn't right.

The knock came once more. The knife stopped.

Edna yanked the door open. Horror. A figure, possibly human, stood before her. The creature's features suggested it was male. His eyes were deep purple with red lines. Darkness silhouetted him. Frost coated his hands and feet, and when he opened his mouth he had no tongue. His black suit spattered with blood told all. He mouthed one word.

"Why?"

Edna's lips trembled and she let out a hysterical sob. The knife sank out of view and her eyes rolled back. Blood squirted onto the hall floor. The grandfather clock let out one long, low tone and fell silent.

Don't, please, don't. I'm leaving now.

Nine

Father

A LOUD KNOCK ON the door woke Liz from her nap. She brushed cookie crumbs off her sweatpants and pushed her bangs to the side, feeling an indent left by her glasses. As her senses returned to her from the black land of dreams, she registered the knock and racked her brain, but she couldn't think of anyone who knew that she had gone up to the family cabin.

She scrunched her eyebrows, looked around the empty room, and placed the book she had been reading entitled Up the Creek on the coffee table. The sound of wind blowing through the treetops and the clicking of cicadas permeated the walls. She stood up from the couch and debated whether to open the door or pretend nobody was home.

Another louder knock interrupted her thoughts, and she remembered her truck was parked right outside, and that anybody with half a brain would know that someone was more than likely inside the cabin. The grandfather clock next to the shuttered window showed it was past five o'clock in the evening. Liz thought it might be a concerned ranger passing through to warn her, and anyone in the neighboring cabins, about the coming storm.

After taking a deep breath, Liz unjammed the heavy door and opened it a few inches. Her father, Gepp, stood on the welcome mat. His long greasy hair was combed, and he was dressed in an ill-fitting pinstriped suit. Liz had never seen her father in anything but jeans and a T-shirt, usually with mechanic gloves hanging from his back pocket. The row of half-dead pine trees behind him complemented his teeth. Liz eyed him warily.

"What are you doing here?" she asked, opening the door a little wider.

"Sorry to intrude on your weekend retreat. Can we talk?" His breath smelled like mint, and there was a shiny gum wrapper on the mat. Gepp covered it with his foot when he noticed Liz was staring at it. She decided not to tell him that a price tag was still attached to his collar and that she could see a package of cigarettes in his breast pocket.

"You still come up here?" Liz asked. She smirked when he didn't look her in the eye.

"Not really. But, I need to talk to you and you weren't at your apartment. Can I come in?"

"You could have called. Unless you prefer intruding."

Gepp bit his lip and turned away for a moment. Liz thought he might leave.

"Can I come in?" He talked so softly, Liz barely heard him.

"Make it quick," she said. She swung the door open and walked away. Gepp closed the door and hung his coat on a nearby hook. He clasped his hands together and chewed his gum loudly while she rearranged the couch cushions.

"I'm sorry you couldn't make it to the funeral," he said.

"I could have. You know that." Liz's tone was ice cold, and her expression matched.

"I don't believe that. I'm sure something kept you." Gepp was looking around the front room, perhaps rethinking his plan to visit.

"I would have come if I'd known you'd corner me anyway," Liz said, her voice raised. "Why are you here?" She threw her hands in the air and stepped toward her father. Gepp ducked past her and stopped without a word. He was looking into the dark fireplace.

"What's in there?" he asked.

"What?" Liz squinted and looked through the moveable metal screen that kept embers from flying out. Gepp moved to the side of the hearth and placed his hand on a built-in drawer next to the mantle.

"Don't you see that lump? It's moving." His piece of gum fell from his mouth as he talked. Liz didn't notice.

She crouched down in front of the hearth and looked more closely. Something small moved in the dark ash causing her to jump. Gepp grabbed one of the fireplace pokers and pushed it through the crack between the brick border and the metal screen. The black lump let out a shriek and unfolded its thin wings.

"Bat," he said. He poked the animal again.

Liz, who had taken a few steps back, watched as the creature attempted to fly up into the chimney and out of sight; it fell down twice before managing to get into hiding. She swallowed; her mouth was dry. "Get it out of here," she whispered. She stepped back.

Gepp pulled a box of matches and some lighter fluid out of the drawer.

"Don't burn it. It's helpless." Her words, and her tone, which might have stopped someone else, went unanswered.

Gepp sprayed the lighter fluid through the screen onto the mass of ashes. Liz couldn't help but think of him as a curious teenager whose parents wouldn't be home from work for another hour. This done, Gepp said, "Don't worry, it'll be fine. The bat will fly out the top when it fills with smoke."

"What if it doesn't?"

Gepp hesitated for a moment, then lit a match and threw it into the fireplace. There was a loud poof, and a flame shot up. The burning ash from the previous fire smelled awful.

"Oh, that's just great."

Gepp grunted.

The fire, if it could be called a fire, had nothing fresh and flammable to burn but the old charred wood, which had been drenched in lighter fluid. Somehow the smoldering heap helped a small flame to spring up and create smoke, which rose into the chimney. Gepp and Liz listened for any hint of the plan having worked. A moment later, screeching filled the cabin. Gepp stared into the smoky fire, and Liz closed her eyes tight.

"Wait, put it out," she said, walking over to the fireplace, her eyes still closed. She was feeling around, about to move the screen when Gepp stepped in the way.

"Stop. We don't want that thing in here. It could be rabid."

Liz opened her eyes. "It's on fire," she screamed.

"And you want it in?"

Liz didn't say anything. They listened until the shrieking stopped and the fire burned down. Gepp took a step back, lifted his boot until he could see the bottom, and used his fingernails to pick at his gum, which had fallen out earlier. The charred and suffocated bat fell into the ashes. "I guess that's over," he said.

"We should put it out. Get some water from the kitchen." Liz moved the screen and used the poker to cover the bat with ash. She heard Gepp go into the kitchen. Her eyes never left the smoky lump. He promptly returned and poured a glass of water over the smoldering corpse.

"Do you have a bag?" he asked.

"Yeah." Liz grabbed a plastic grocery bag from the coffee table and emptied out several boxes of cookies before handing it to Gepp.

"Thanks." He placed the bat in the bag and took it outside. The wind had started to really howl. Liz sat down on the couch. When Gepp came back in, he sat on the recliner across from her. The chairs stood only a few feet apart. Nobody talked until the clock struck six, emitting a metallic noise. It was about this time that it started to rain.

"Why are you here?" she asked.

Gepp sighed and glanced around the room. "Is that new?" he asked, nodding his head toward the corner. Liz turned and saw the painting she had bought earlier that day leaning under the window. Raindrop shadows ran along the shutters and across the adjacent wall.

"Yeah, it's for my apartment. Like it?" she asked.

"Where'd you get it?"

"The flea market downtown."

Gepp nodded his head and looked at the painting. The gray and black strokes ran along hints of yellow to form an abstract image. Liz watched Gepp lose himself in the painting for several minutes.

"Why did you come?" she repeated.

"How much was it?"

Liz stared.

"All right. I actually came to give you this," Gepp said, producing a leather-bound book from his back pocket, which had been wrapped in twine. Liz leaned forward and grabbed it before he had a chance to give it to her.

"Where did you get this? I lost this years ago."

Gepp cleared his throat and took a deep breath. "I cleaned out the attic after the funeral. Your mother always loved holding onto things."

"Did you read it?"

"I thought it was one of her old diaries. Don't worry. I stopped at the bottom of the first page where you wrote, 'I hate dad.'" He stared at the ground.

"I'm sorry." She didn't know why she felt the need to apologize. She knew she hadn't done anything wrong. Gepp was the one who needed to be apologizing.

She watched him shake his head. "I'm the one who's sorry," he said. "And I mean for more than reading that." He gestured to the diary.

Liz knew what he meant. She placed her head in her hands and said, "I want her back."

"I miss her too." The conversation lulled. Gepp flared his nostrils and continued looking down. "Do you blame me?"

Liz stared at him until he looked up. "I did." She pursed her lips.

"Do you still?" he asked, never losing eye contact.

Liz wanted to give an honest answer. Her lips relaxed. "I don't know."

After a moment, Gepp put his hands together, leaned forward, and looked at Liz.

"I blame my— I will always blame myself. She was drunk, and I let her get behind the wheel and go." His voice caught. "I'm sorry... every day, for that fight. I don't want to fight anymore."

Liz didn't say anything; she was leafing through her diary. Gepp watched her, being careful to not look at the open pages she was obviously lost in. The sounds of wind and rain grew louder and louder.

"I better go," Gepp said.

"Wait." Liz grabbed the book she had been reading, Up the Creek, and extended it to him. Her diary remained open on her lap, and an old black-and-white family photo was visible in the center of it. Liz, as a small child, stood between her parents, holding their hands. "I'll let you stay," she said, "if you'll read to me."

Gepp tilted his head to the side. "Really? It's been a while."

"Really. You can't drive home in that. Mom wouldn't let you. And, I'm too tired to read."

Gepp cautiously extended his hand and grabbed the book. He turned it over in his hands. "I've never read this. You'll have to fill me in."

Liz closed her diary and scooted over on the couch. "You'll pick up on it."

Gepp moved to the couch and opened the book. Liz smiled at the price tag hanging from his collar and the package of cigarettes in his breast pocket. She pulled a small blanket over her feet, closed her eyes, and listened.

Ten

Waiting for a Train

EVERYTHING ON THE TRAIN platform was either gray or black. The lamp posts, signs, benches, rails, payphone, and automated ticket kiosk were black. The platform floor, bench enclosures, rail curb, and sign lettering were gray.

The platform itself was small, situated between a parking lot and a long line of dismal-looking row homes. The sky above was cloudy and a slight breeze was whipping along the ground at an annoyingly constant speed.

Gabby, the only person on the platform, was dressed in a faded black overcoat and jeans. She was sitting on a bench, waiting for the train to rattle down the tracks and take her away. Her mouth and chin were wrapped in a burgundy scarf, more so to keep the filthy, polluted air out of her lungs than to keep her face warm.

It was the holiday season, and she was going to her mother's house in the country. Her arms were clasped tightly around her torso and her right leg was bouncing up and down in small, vibrative movements.

As she sat there waiting, she tried to remember what color the train was that usually picked her up. She couldn't remember but decided that it was most likely either white or dirty-white depending on the time of day.

She checked her watch. The time was five minutes past the hour, which meant that the train was running late.

She stood up and paced between the benches, looking down the track every few seconds. Just after completing her fourth trip up and down the short section of the platform, she stopped.

There was a man clad in black approaching her from the platform entrance. He was holding a stubby, black pistol and it was pointed her way.

She didn't know what to do. Should she run? If she ran, would he shoot? She waited for him to get closer.

"Who are you?" she asked.

He smiled with his lips. "Come with me," he said, gesturing with his gun.

His voice was higher pitched than Gabby had expected; which, for some reason, terrified her a great deal.

The two of them stared at each other for a long moment. The man had gray eyes and black hair. His face looked surprisingly happy, perhaps because of his chubby, red cheeks.

Afraid to go with the man, Gabby decided that fighting him—catching him off guard—was her best option. Images of the self-defense class she had taken at the recreation center during the summer months flashed through her mind. Most of them involved her standing around watching everybody else kick and hit each other with padded mitts. It wasn't a particularly good memory.

She bit her lip, nodded her head, and took a step toward the man. Before her fist had moved half an inch, the man pushed the pistol into her side and grabbed her arm. She froze. What in the world was she doing? He had a gun.

"Careful. You wouldn't want something to happen to your dear, sweet mother," he said. Gabby, who had been fighting gravity, let her body go limp in the man's arms. The gun barrel continued to push into her side.

"What? Who are you?" she asked.

A low whistle and a slight rumble betrayed the train approaching the platform. The man waited, clutching Gabby close to him.

The train came to a gentle stop in front of the two pedestrians. The doors opened and a small group of people walked off the train and onto the platform.

Gabby blinked; and, just like that, the man with the gun was gone. She hadn't felt him leave.

Where had he gone? She looked up and down the platform, looked through the train's windows, but he was nowhere to be seen.

Deciding that the man was certainly not on the platform and that he still might have gotten on the train, Gabby took a step toward the open doors, but it was too late. The doors slid closed before she reached them.

She ran forward and pounded on the doors. Nobody was on the inside of the train, it seemed, to open the doors for her. The train started to move, slowly at first, then faster and faster.

Gabby chased after it until she reached the end of the platform. It turned slightly on the track before disappearing from view. Gabby watched it go.

She needed to get ahold of her mother. The man in black had threatened her, after all.

Gabby pulled her cellphone out of her jeans pocket. The battery was dead. She caught sight of a payphone at the center of the platform and hurriedly went over to it. She went to grab the receiver, but there wasn't one. A frayed silver conduit hung loosely to the side of the beat-up old payphone box.

Without thinking, Gabby kicked the base of the payphone, then she immediately regretted it. She blinked away tears and looked around the platform, hoping to find somebody with a phone that she could borrow, but she was the only person there.

She ran into the parking lot. It was vacant as well. A low whistle and slight rumble told of another approaching train. She raced back onto the platform and waited, not wanting to let this train depart without her on it.

She stepped up to the grayish-yellow painted caution line and stared at the oncoming train. Its headlights were on despite the sun still hanging over the horizon. The train looked like a long metal snake; and, Gabby realized, it wasn't slowing down.

She started waving her arms frantically, but there was nobody in the conductor's box to see her. The train seemed to pick up speed as it flew past her.

"Leave, then!" she shouted as it whipped by her.

The train disappeared around the bend. How long had it been since the man had come and gone? Too long.

Gabby knew she needed to find another way to get to her mother's.

She left the platform, walked through the parking lot, and came to the deserted bus stop. Where in the world was everybody? She checked the posted bus schedule and saw that there should have been a bus there at that exact moment.

Gabby sat down on the curb. A tear fell from her cheek. She would wake up at any moment. She knew she would. She was already at her mother's house asleep on the couch.

Another low whistle and rumble told of a third approaching train. Gabby slowly turned her head and stared at the train. This time, it slowed down.

She sprang up about to run when she saw the man with the gun standing on the platform. Once again, she didn't know what to do. She could run this time; she was far enough away. The man motioned for her to come over by jerking his head to the side.

Gabby started walking, but she was immediately stopped. People came out of everywhere. So many people. They stepped out from behind parked cars, low cement walls, and metal trash cans. Several of them were holding large, black video cameras.

A woman wearing a coat the color of olives walked up to Gabby, microphone in hand. She looked familiar: from the TV, maybe.

"You're Gabby, right?" asked the woman.

Her voice certainly sounded like it was from a television show. Gabby noticed that she was talking into the microphone and now holding the microphone out to her.

"Yes," replied Gabby.

"You've been set up!" yelled the woman. "It was your mom. She called us!"

All the people cheered and laughed. The man with the gun was now standing beside her. "How're you feeling?" he asked, a big, toothy smile on his face. "Your mom is right there." He pointed the gun at an elderly woman standing a few feet away, waving her arm. He pulled the trigger and a stream of water shot out.

Gabby felt like she was going to faint. Her eyes closed; the world darkened. Somebody would catch her.

Eleven

Between Chips and Chocolate

WHEN ANGIE LEFT HER apartment for work around four in the afternoon, she read the yellow note which she had stuck to the back of her front door the night before: "Get the promotion!"

Even though she had been drinking when she had written it, now that she was sober, she still felt like it would happen. Today was the day.

She was driving to work as she remembered the note, and the black Mercedes in front of her came up short, forcing her to slam on her brakes. She immediately forgot about the note and everything else in her life.

Somewhere, a horn blared.

On instinct, she glanced in the rearview mirror to see if anyone was about to slam into her car, but the tan SUV behind her had already managed to stop.

Angie honked her horn and shook her head a little. Today was supposed to be a good day, and she wasn't about to let a little traffic get in the way. She would need to apologize to her boss, Jim, when she arrived late. This would only be the third time in a year and a half. It wouldn't ruin her chances; she wouldn't let it.

When she did arrive at Jim's Oddities, nobody appeared to be in the store, and there was a strong smell of something burning coming from the back. The front room was filled with the same junk as always, although Jim never called it that. He always referred to everything as "treasure".

Angie entered the small back room and gasped. Jim was lying on the floor, face down. His head was cocked to the side so that she couldn't see his expression. There was no apparent blood, and the body didn't seem to be moving.

As soon as she realized what was happening, she pulled out her phone and dialed 911. She hoped that it wasn't too late, but there was a sinking feeling in the pit of her stomach like a chunk of ice had somehow appeared there without her knowing.

The police came quickly. In the meantime, she didn't approach the body. She wanted to, kind of, but she was afraid. When the front door banged open, she left the room and sat on an antique chair near the cash register.

One of the responding officers turned off the oven and removed the burnt food, whatever it was, shortly after arriving. The burning smell. She had almost forgotten.

Two weeks later, Angie found herself sitting in the main office of Dependable & Durable Boxes Inc. It was a box manufacturing facility where her brother worked, and where she had now worked for three days. The work was monotonous, but it promised to keep her bank account from reaching zero anytime soon.

It had only taken two days for Jim's Oddities to close down, thanks to Jim's kids. Angie bit her lip as she thought about the old store and her old life. Funny, how things had stayed the same for years, then changed so rapidly in a moment. A heart attack, she thought. A short burst of air escaped her nostrils.

Mr. Mino, Angie's new boss, sat across from her at his desk, shuffling through some papers. He placed a paper clip over a few sheets and set them down in front of him. He didn't look particularly happy; then again, Angie had never seen him look any other way. He clasped his hands together and looked up.

"Thank you for coming, Angie. I'm afraid I have some bad news. Human resources sent me a letter this morning, and it contained a complaint regarding your employment." He paused for a moment before continuing. "I'll be blunt. The situation isn't very good."

Angie didn't know what to think. She couldn't imagine anything that she had done in the past three days that would warrant a complaint. "A complaint, sir?"

She had never called Mr. Mino "sir" before, and he smiled a little. He caught her eye, glanced away, returned to his normal almost mad self, and looked back at her.

"I'm sorry, Angie." His thumb tapped against the end of his pointer finger. "I didn't know this when I hired you, but apparently immediate family members can't be employed in the same warehouse.

"You see, I've never had to deal with this before... Anyway, since our next nearest warehouse is one hundred and twenty miles away, I'm afraid that means we are going to have to let you go."

"You mean, I don't have a job because of a stup—because of some rule?" She couldn't believe what she was hearing. No, she thought, the situation didn't look good.

"I'm afraid so," replied Mr. Mino. His thumb stopped tapping and he tried to smile once more. He slid the papers with the paper clip across the table so that she could see them. In big, bold letters at the top of the first paper, it read: "Termination Notice".

"I'm sorry," he added. There wasn't much more to say.

Angie didn't grab the notice; she stood up and left. Mr. Mino didn't stop her.

Three days later, on Saturday night, Angie found herself standing in the middle of a gas station. She had been there for a little over five minutes, and to everyone who passed by her, she looked like she was debating between chips and chocolate.

Nobody noticed her nervous tick, her fingers, which slowly gripped and tugged at her jeans, nor did they notice her eyes, which shifted between the cash register and the junk food in front of her.

A life was about to change forever, and the only person who knew it didn't even know it. For her to have known it, she would have needed to be much less involved in her own daily affairs, but she wasn't. Her daily affairs were all that she had, and they hadn't been going well lately.

So, she sat and pondered between chips and chocolate; and, maybe, somewhere, changing her life in a moment.

It wasn't too much longer before she took a step toward the counter, but she stopped. The man who wore a red vest and worked at the gas station was coming out of the backroom, and he was holding a sign.

It was a "Help Wanted" sign.

"Hey," she heard herself say loudly. She checked her volume and said, "I can help."

The man looked confused for a moment, then he looked down at the sign he was holding, and his expression changed. He looked back up and stared at Angie. Perhaps, he was waiting for her to say something else.

She didn't say another word, but she also didn't break eye contact. There was something inexpressible in the space between them.

The man lowered the sign to his side.

"Well, come on then."

Twelve

Bonus: Missing: The Morris Mysteries #1

MY PARENTS NAMED ME Evan Morris. They died when I was fifteen years old. I remember when the doctor told me about their deaths, I punched the hospital wall and cried in the hallway. He didn't try to prepare me for the heart-wrenching news that would change my life forever. He didn't sit me down. There wasn't a moment of hesitation on his part. He just stated their demise, plain and simple.

"Their deaths were sudden," he said. "They stalled on the tracks and the train couldn't stop in time. I'm sorry."

I stared at him after he said that. Just for a moment. Of course, I wasn't really looking at him. I was looking at my life through a microscope. Everything was fuzzy and bulbous—I think it was a blur of memory. I remember seeing red. I didn't feel pain when my knuckles hit the wall, but my hand did start to bleed and somebody put a bandage on it.

The doctor left me with a tall social worker who drove me to a cramped brick building on the edge of town where I fell asleep. On the car ride over, I was asked if I wanted to talk, but I didn't. I don't remember anything else about that day. All the days that followed were a similar haze of emotionless faces and lengthy meetings. Mostly, for grief counseling.

Without any siblings or nearby relatives, I was left alone in the world.

After a month of waiting in the custody of the state, I traveled eight hundred miles across the country to live with my Uncle Cecil: my only living relative. The majority of my journey was made by rail because nobody wanted to drive me and there were no airports near the small western town where he was currently living. I was told that he traveled frequently for his job.

"What does he do for a living?" I asked the social worker on my last day in the cramped brick building.

"He'll be able to tell you more than I can. Some sort of freelancer or contractor."

I didn't press for more details.

The train ride took three days. I rode alone in an empty compartment, never venturing out except to use the shared bathroom. The train was almost completely empty. The rest of the passengers seemed keen to keep to themselves. That was fine by me.

Food arrived just inside my doorway three times a day. Whenever the train stopped, I simply glanced out the window to see where we were. Mostly, I saw a lot of dirt and sagebrush with the occasional rural building off in the distance.

Before I had left the city, the tall social worker assured me that my uncle would be waiting for me when I got off the train. However, when I arrived on the dusty platform, there was not another soul in sight. A few buildings ran along a street not far from the platform, but it was difficult to tell what they were because I could only see their backends. Not knowing what else to do, I sat down on one of the wooden benches.

About an hour went by.

I was staring at a prickly cactus just off the edge of the platform when a voice startled me.

"Interesting plants, huh?"

I turned to see a girl sitting on the edge of the bench. She looked taller than me and had long black hair tied into a ponytail. I thought her skin looked incredibly white for someone sitting in the middle of the desert. I wondered where she had come from.

"Yeah," I said. "Very interesting."

I tried to think of something else to say, but my mind went blank. She didn't wait for me to come up with a new subject, though. As if she could read my mind, she answered the questions I didn't even know I had.

"I'm Jeanne, and I live here. Here, meaning Oaks Cliff—not off in the boonies." She looked around the empty platform. "Not that there's much to do here." She turned back to look at me. "Whenever I'm bored, I come to the train station, looking for new people." She cocked her head to one side, and I felt like I needed to tell her my name.

"I'm Evan."

"I like it. It fits you perfectly. I hope you don't mind that I say so. You just look like an Evan." She hesitated for a moment, then added, "Maybe this is totally random, but do you want to get something to eat?"

"I'm waiting for my uncle," I replied without thinking.

I'd been waiting for an hour already and I was starving. I also thought Jeanne was nice. I wanted to know more about her, and here she was giving me every opportunity. I hoped she wouldn't let my lame excuse send her away.

"The diner is right there," she said, nodding toward a small rectangular building not more than one hundred yards away. "I'm sure he'll find you without any trouble."

She stood up and smiled. My stomach made an attempt to leap into my throat. She was odd, I knew that, but for the first time since my parents' deaths, I didn't want to be alone.

Even though I had meant to wait on the train platform until my uncle arrived, I had not expected a girl to ask me to come with her. I lifted my suitcase and accompanied her off the platform. As we walked, I thought she would bombard me with questions about where I was from and what I was doing in town, but she said nothing at all. She didn't act like anyone I had ever known before. That was my first impression of her. Different.

We arrived at the diner and Jeanne excused herself to go to the restroom. I found a booth and sat down. It was becoming painfully obvious to me that I didn't know how to talk to girls. I sat awkwardly in the booth and waited for her to return, thinking about what I would say when she did. Nothing came to mind.

That's when a man with brown hair and a tan jacket slid into the seat across from me. Nobody had to tell me he was my uncle. He had the same round nose and small ears as my father.

"Evan Morris," he said. "I expected to meet you at the train station. Sorry I was a bit late. Need me to buy you something to eat?"

He smiled at me and leaned forward as though we knew each other. I had the odd sensation that I was staring at my father. He raised his eyebrows and sniffed. He might have had the beginning or ending stages of a cold.

"Sorry about leaving the station," I said. "And, I'm not really hungry."

I didn't know whether or not to tell him I was waiting for Jeanne. It already seemed like a strange enough meeting since I had never actually met my uncle before. Several seconds passed. I opened my mouth to try and tell him about meeting someone at the train station when Jeanne walked up and extended her hand to him.

"Hello. I'm Jeanne," she said in a cheery tone.

My uncle sat up and shook her hand.

"Hello to you too." He glanced at me. "Am I in the middle of something?" he asked.

"We met at the train station," I said.

Jeanne sat down next to me. She smelled like perfume. Judging by the way my uncle's nostrils flared, he smelled it too. He was smiling at me with his hands clasped together on the table. I had no idea what he was thinking.

"I hope I didn't get Evan in trouble by bringing him here," said Jeanne. "I figured you of all people could find him without any problem."

"Ah. I see that I've been recognized. But, no. It's never too difficult to track someone down, especially when there is food nearby."

My uncle winked at me, but I was completely lost.

"Um... Uncle Cecil, what—" I began.

"Just Cecil. There is no point in you always referring to me as uncle. It makes me feel old. Not that it would be too much of an issue if you really wanted to call me that. Either way, I suppose. I'll leave it up to you. Sorry, what were you saying?"

"Er... I can't remember now..."

"No problem. I'm sure you'll think of it eventually. In fact, I'm sure we'll have plenty of time to chat later."

Cecil glanced at a golden wristwatch and looked from me to Jeanne then back to me.

"I'm sorry, but I need to get back to the motel to do some work. You can meet me there right after you've eaten. Jeanne, you're welcome to come. It's the motel next door. Room 118."

I tried to say something. I'm not sure exactly what. It seemed wrong to let him leave when we had only just met. He put up his hand as he walked away from the table, repeating for me not to worry and to enjoy myself.

I turned back to Jeanne. She didn't move to the other side of the table.

"I told you he would find you here," she said.

A waitress walked over with two plates of food. She placed a club sandwich in front of me and walked back behind the counter. Jeanne had the exact same sandwich in front of her.

"Sorry if you don't like it. I ordered just as you found a place to sit. Also, don't worry about paying. You're new here."

"Thanks. It looks good."

I didn't know what else to add, so I took a bite of sandwich and realized how hungry I was. It was only a matter of minutes before my food was completely gone. Jeanne was about halfway done. She had yet to bombard me with questions.

"Do you know my uncle?" I asked, remembering what I meant to ask Cecil before he left.

"No, not personally. I've just read the paper and heard things from friends and family. People who knew him back when he was growing up here. Is it really all true, though?"

I felt stupid for not knowing what she was talking about. I felt my face getting warm.

"Um... What?"

Jeanne waved her hand and said, "You don't have to answer that. I didn't mean to be rude."

I decided to change the subject.

"Tell me something about you."

"Me? I'm not interesting. I've lived here my whole life. I walk around town a lot. Nature is cool, I guess. I used to have a camera and I took a lot of pictures."

"That's cool. What happened to it?"

"I dropped it while climbing a pile of rocks to get a picture of the sunset," she said.

"Oh. I'm sorry."

"It's okay. I was still able to get the photos off the memory card. I might be able to fix it one day if I can bring myself to try to figure out the problem."

"I hope you figure it out. What do you do now that you can't take pictures?"

"Follow the news, I guess. I'm trying my hand at writing. Journalism is kind of cool."

"Is there a lot of news here?"

I didn't mean to sound rude, but I thought I might have. Luckily, Jeanne laughed and pushed the remaining part of her sandwich away.

"It's funny that you should ask. I mean, your uncle is here, right? He doesn't just show up out of the blue to no-news towns. At first, I thought he was visiting old friends, but then I heard the story."

"What story?"

"You mean you don't know? The Paz's son went missing. Paul. At least, that's what I heard. I don't know any details yet because the family is keeping it as quiet as possible. Well, as quiet as they can, seeing as how they are the richest family in town."

"What does Cecil have to do—" I began to ask, but was stopped when the waitress returned. She picked up the plates and walked away.

Jeanne slid out of the booth.

"I should get going. Sorry, but I just realized what time it is. I'll see you tomorrow, okay?"

Before I could say anything, she left the diner. I got up, grabbed my suitcase, and walked out too. It was almost dark. Jeanne was nowhere to be seen. I hoped I hadn't said anything to make her leave.

I walked to the motel, which was easy to find because of the large sign out front. It was on the other side of the diner just as Cecil had said it would be. I passed a small but well-lit lobby on the first floor. Looking through the glass doors, I saw a vacant registration counter with a silver bell in the center. I could tell that the motel did not get many guests.

I made my way along the long line of doors until I reached 118. I knocked and waited, hoping that I had reached the right room. I thought about knocking again when nobody answered for more than a minute, then the door opened and Cecil greeted me.

"Hello again," he said. "Sorry for not answering sooner. I was finishing a note."

He motioned for me to step inside and I wheeled in my suitcase. Cecil closed the door and pointed to the far bed.

"You'll be sleeping there. First time I've gotten two beds in a room, you know? Not that I mind. The more the merrier, right?"

I was watching him as he talked. He wasn't standing still; he was doing things. There were papers and folders on top of the desk next to the window. He shuffled these around, flipping papers over and shoving notes under manila envelopes. I realized I still didn't know what it was that he did for a living.

"What are you working on?" I asked.

"Just another missing person. Should be cleared up in a matter of days. Nothing too terribly exciting, but the pay seems good. I'm hoping for something trickier once we move farther west. Sorry about the motel living by the way. You get used to it."

He finished rearranging his desk and turned toward me.

Seeing my puzzled expression, he asked, "Is everything alright?"

"Um... Yes. I just didn't understand everything. What about a missing person?"

Cecil raised his eyebrows and said, "The missing person I'm investigating."

"You investigate missing people?"

"Missing people? Yes. I also investigate anything that needs my attention. That's why they call me an investigator, after all."

I was shocked.

"There's a missing person and you're going to find them? Like in a movie?" I asked.

He smiled and nodded.

"Something like that. Yes. You know, I'm surprised nobody told you. Did your parents... well, I shouldn't really ask."

"No. It's okay. And, I'm sorry. They never mentioned it. Can I ask you why Jeanne knew who you were at the diner? Are you famous?"

Cecil shook his head and said, "No. I wouldn't say famous. I've just shown up in the newspaper a few times. Anyone who still reads to get their news may have heard of me."

"I guess that makes sense," I said. "So, who is this Paul Paz person you're looking into? I heard you were hired by some rich people to find him. Is he famous too?"

"All of the Pazes are well-known in this area because of their wealth but none of them are famous. In fact, I don't think I know any famous people. As far as their son Paul goes, yes, he is missing, and yes, I was hired to help find him. I was also told to be discreet about it, so I'd rather not go into too much detail right now. I only just started investigating today after all."

The streetlights in the parking lot flickered on, illuminating the window.

"You must be exhausted from traveling," Cecil said. "How about you settle in for the night and we can talk more about, well, everything, in the morning."

Once in bed, I felt like tossing and turning, but I stayed motionless to avoid disturbing Cecil. Even though he had hinted at being done with work for the night, he was still sitting at the desk reading through some of his papers. Every few minutes I would hear him pick up a new document. He grunted or hummed occasionally.

I don't know how many hours passed while I listened to him work. My brain continually jumped from one thought to the next. I played the scene from the diner over and over again in my head. Had Jeanne really been there? Why was she so friendly? I tried to not overthink it. Part of me was still in shock from learning about Cecil's career.

Just as my mind started to unwind and I thought I might be able to finally fall asleep, there was a knock at the door. I kept my eyes mostly closed and stayed motionless. Cecil turned and looked at me for a moment before checking the peephole and opening the door.

"Neal? What do you want?" he asked.

"How is your case coming?" a man responded.

His voice traveled more through his nose than his mouth. Even though it was dark outside and I barely had my eyes open, I could see the visitor's badge. He was a police officer.

"Better if I could get back to it," said my uncle.

"Working on it into the night? Maybe you should get some rest and come back to it tomorrow. It's only been a day after all. Not to mention, you sure you should be working now that you have another person to look after? Babysitting sure sounds fun."

The officer stood a little taller and looked over Cecil's shoulder. My uncle moved the door and stood up in the officer's line of sight.

"Don't need anything? Good."

The door closed.

I thought I heard the officer chuckle. Cecil shook his head and returned to the desk. I couldn't make heads or tails of what I had just seen. I tried for a few minutes to connect the conversation to what I knew about my uncle, but I gave up before too long. I began to doze off again. I don't know how much time passed, but I was startled awake when the motel door closed.

I sat up and looked around. Cecil had gone.

I got out of bed, got dressed in the clothes I had been wearing earlier, and left the motel room. The door closed behind me and I regretted not grabbing a keycard, but it was too late. I noticed that the air was much cooler now than it had been during the day.

Two street lights lit the parking lot, making it difficult to see anything past the edge of the motel's property. Luckily, I spotted Cecil between the motel and the diner before he left the circle of light. I recognized his tan coat. He was alone and moving rather quickly. I followed him into the darkness, keeping track of only his silhouette against the limited street lights.

He made his way to the front of the diner. I quietly crossed the street so he wouldn't see me and crouched behind a bush. Apparently, I was not stealthy enough because he turned and waved to me a moment after I stopped moving. I didn't know what to do, so I continued to stay behind the bush. He shook his head and I thought I saw a smile on his face, although, that was probably my imagination because it was difficult to see details from across the street.

He made his way to me and stood next to the bush.

"I can see that you're going to be a handful. Why don't you step out of the bush and come with me into the diner?"

I got out from behind the bush.

"I'm sorry."

"Don't be sorry. This is all new to you and I left you alone." He caught my eye and I felt something ineffable pass between us. I smiled, glad that Cecil wasn't chewing me out for following him through an unfamiliar town at night.

He stepped back into the road and I followed him into the empty diner. We sat in the corner booth and Cecil ordered us both pancakes and eggs. He watched the door as we waited for our food.

"What are we doing here?" I asked.

"I'm meeting with my client. You're here to eat."

He checked his watch and returned to looking at the door.

"Should I sit somewhere else?"

I wasn't sure if I wanted to meet a client who couldn't meet during the day.

"I don't mind if you sit here. Just, don't say anything when they arrive."

Our food was brought out and a few seconds later a well-dressed couple entered the diner. There were no other customers as far as I could see. The man had slicked-back hair and a thin mustache. The woman was tall with a plain face. They walked over to our booth and sat down. The man looked at me and I glanced down at the table.

"Glenda and Monty, I'm glad you could meet. Would you like anything?" my uncle asked.

"No, thank you. Is this your nephew? Officer Neal mentioned him during our meeting earlier today," said Mr. Paz.

"Yes, this is Evan. I hope you don't mind that he tagged along. He was hungry."

I looked at the man and he flashed a quick smile.

"Not at all. Two heads are better than one, right? How old are you, Evan?"

"Nearly fifteen," I said, glancing at Cecil when I remembered he had asked me not to talk.

"Wonderful age," said Mrs. Paz, while Mr. Paz nodded.

With every minute that passed, I felt more lost. I gathered that Mr. and Mrs. Paz were my uncle's clients, but I had no idea what was being discussed. As curious as I had been moments before, I wished to be anywhere else now that everyone was here. I should have felt like I was on the sidelines, watching Cecil do his job. Instead, I felt like I was in the middle of something I didn't want to be in the middle of.

"Perfect. Well, whenever you're ready. I'm all ears," my uncle said.

"I'll just start with early Tuesday afternoon," began Mr. Paz. "That's the last time I saw Paul. He was working in the yard. I was leaving for the office because of a meeting. Glenda was at home with a horrible migraine, laying in the bedroom."

Mrs. Paz nodded her head but didn't speak.

"Was Paul alone when he was working in the yard?" asked my uncle.

"As far as I know, yes. Granted somebody could have been around. I had no reason to think anything of guests at the time."

"Of course. Continue."

"I drove to the office and had my meeting which went as planned. It was about an hour later that I returned home. I went upstairs to comfort my wife, then I asked what Paul was doing. She didn't know, so I went looking for him in the yard. I didn't find him. When I noticed that he had also left several of the tools out, I began to worry. He'd never do that."

"Is it possible that he went away with some friends without telling you?" asked my uncle.

"If that did happen, it would be the first time. He was such a good boy. He is a good boy. I just want him to come home safely."

"What did the police do when you told them?"

"They didn't do enough. I don't even know why I bothered going to them. I should have come straight to you. I didn't even think about that, though."

"Going to the police was the right thing to do, incompetent though Neal might be. It may prove useful later to have that paperwork filed. We can always call on the force when we really need help. Has Neal said anything to you about the case since then?"

"He's found nothing."

"Thank you," said Cecil. "That's all I need to know for now. I'll let you know when I learn more. You will hear from me tomorrow afternoon at the latest. With a little bit of luck, all of this can be resolved before the week is out."

I couldn't believe my ears and I almost forgot that I wasn't supposed to talk, but I stayed quiet and watched as Cecil shook hands with the Pazes. It was a shorter conversation than I had expected. Even though I didn't know him, I hoped Paul was safe, wherever he was.

"I trust you'll track him down quickly. Thank you again," said Mr. Paz.

Mrs. Paz stood up and I watched as the two of them left. As far as I could tell, they did not get in a car. I figured that they lived close enough to walk. Cecil, who had barely touched his food, ate quickly, then we left.

The following morning, I woke to find my uncle dressed and ready for the day. He was about to leave when he noticed I was awake. He smiled and tapped his finger on a piece of paper on the desk.

"I left a note this time. I'm going out for a bit."

"Where are you going?"

"The north end of town. Got a call about a potential lead. I'll be back in a few hours."

"Wait, and I'll come with you."

He put his hands in his pockets and looked at me with a half-smile.

"I'm afraid you can't. Not because I don't want you to. People are just less likely to answer me if I bring a guest. Stay here and I'll fill you in when I come back for lunch. It will be nice to have someone to bounce ideas off of for once."

He left, pulling the door shut behind him. I got up and walked over to the window. There were two sets of curtains which I pulled aside. Cecil drove away in a white rental car, leaving me alone for the foreseeable future. I quickly showered and put on one of the two pairs of clothes that I had brought. Then, I sat down on the edge of my bed. Boredom set in almost immediately.

My uncle's suitcase lay at the foot of his bed, closed but unzipped. Wanting to know more about him, I lifted the front flap. Unsurprisingly, the majority of the main compartment was filled with clothes. He had a few dress shirts, some T-shirts, and a few pairs of jeans and slacks. I closed the flap and unzipped one of the side pockets. Inside, there was a packet of mint gum and two ticket stubs to a basketball game. I didn't recognize the team names.

Not wanting to snoop too much, I zipped the pocket up and left the suitcase as I had found it. Looking around I saw he had also left behind his tan jacket and a pair of tennis shoes. The jacket was completely empty as were the tennis shoes. I sat back down on the edge of my bed, feeling a little guilty about my nosy behavior. I had learned almost nothing.

That's when my mind started to wander and I thought back to the conversation Mr. Paz and Cecil had had the night before. A part of me was surprised by the whole situation I had found myself in. Another part of me liked the idea of living and traveling with a private investigator.

I thought about school and what would happen once summer was over. Would Cecil stop traveling so I could remain at the same school? Would I never make friends again because of his need to travel? These thoughts drove me to want some fresh air. I left the room and walked to the center of the parking lot.

I leaned on one of the streetlights and thought about what to do while I waited for Cecil to return. Going for a long walk was the most obvious answer. I could explore the town and see if there was anything interesting. A part of me wanted to run into Jeanne again so I could ask her for a phone number. I hadn't had the courage the night before.

As luck would have it, I saw Jeanne walking across the nearly empty parking lot toward me. She smiled and waved when she noticed I was staring at her. I couldn't believe my luck. I wondered if I was the reason that she was near the motel. I hoped so.

"What are you doing?" she asked when she got near enough.

"I don't know. Cecil left so I came out here."

I couldn't believe how stupid I sounded. How could I not know what I was doing? I probably looked like a creep just standing around the parking lot by myself. I smiled at Jeanne and pretended like I wasn't internally cringing.

"If you want, you can come with me to the river. It's a nice place to sit and relax."

"Great. Let's go," I said, not wanting to question where a river would be in the desert.

I knew I shouldn't go. Cecil was expecting me to wait at the motel. I hardly knew him, though, and I wanted to spend time with Jeanne. I justified my leaving because he had had the opportunity to take me with him before he left.

I walked to the edge of the parking lot with Jeanne when a police car turned down the street toward us. Its blue and red lights turned on unaccompanied by the siren. I stopped and waited to see what the cruiser would do. It pulled up alongside where we were standing. I looked in the driver's seat and recognized the officer from the night before.

He got out of the car and walked over to me.

"Can you tell me why your friend ran away?" he asked.

I looked to my left and saw that Jeanne was no longer anywhere in sight. She had run off without a word. My throat was dry as I turned back to look at the officer.

"I really don't know," I said.

"It looks to me like the two of you were loitering. Too bad you didn't have the sense to join your friend, wherever she went."

"I didn't need to join her. I wasn't doing anything wrong."

"Maybe. Maybe not. Either way, you need to come to the station."

"I'm being arrested?" I asked.

"I didn't say that. I just need you to come and answer some questions."

I thought about running, but I didn't have anywhere to go. Besides, I truly hadn't done anything wrong. I got into the back of the police car without arguing. There was no need to give the officer a legitimate reason to arrest me.

The station was only three blocks to the north. We rode in silence. When we arrived, Officer Neal opened my door and motioned for me to get out. He didn't touch me and never said anything. There was nobody at the front desk when we entered the station. I stood by the front door while the officer walked into an office in the corner. A moment later, he came back with a pen and clipboard.

"You're Evan, correct? The Morris nephew?"

"Yes. Who are you?"

"I'm Officer Neal Scott. Do you mind if we talk about your uncle for a few minutes?"

I wondered for a moment what would happen if I said no. He would most likely carry on with the conversation anyway. I decided to play along.

"I guess so. Can I ask why you visited him last night?"

Officer Neal smiled. He most likely didn't know that I had been awake.

"We're old friends and I heard that he was in town. Do you know what your uncle does for a living?"

"He's a private investigator, or I guess that's what he's called."

I hadn't thought much about what Cecil's job title would be. He was just a guy with a tan coat who met with people and asked them questions.

"That's right. Did he ever tell you about how he became a crack detective?"

This question seemed odd and I had no idea how to answer.

"No. I only met him yesterday. I've never been this far west before."

Officer Neal raised his eyebrows and scribbled something on his clipboard.

"Interesting. Your parents died recently, correct? Why didn't they introduce you to your uncle before?"

A lump formed in my stomach. I hadn't expected questions that involved my parents.

"I'm not really sure. I guess he just wasn't ever in the neighborhood. My parents didn't travel much, so we just never crossed paths."

Officer Neal stared at me and made sure I was looking at him before he asked his next question.

"Are you sure your parents weren't trying to protect you from him?"

I was shocked.

"What do you mean?"

I thought I saw a smile momentarily on the officer's face.

"I don't know if I should be the one to tell you this, but I don't think there is anyone else who would. Before Cecil became an annoyance to the police by investigating crimes on his own behalf, he was an officer in this town."

"How does that make him someone my parents wouldn't want me to see?"

"That's just it. That alone doesn't. It's how he left the force that would make you reconsider spending time with him."

"What happened?" I asked.

He killed a man. Just in front of this station. Shot him in the middle of the street. Shot him in the back while he was running."

I unintentionally smirked. This bit of news seemed like a lie. I was hardly phased, and I could tell that Officer Neal was disappointed by my reaction.

"If that were true, wouldn't he be in jail?" I asked.

"Self-defense. One of the fastest, overlooked cases in our state's history. No media coverage. Swept under the rug like nothing happened. Sadly, these things occur."

"You said that he killed a man, but you didn't say murder. Why did he shoot? Maybe it was self-defense after all."

Officer Neal bit his front lip and said, "I should have said murder. I guess I was just used to how the paperwork was worded after the incident. It was most definitely not self-defense."

I could tell that I was bugging Officer Neal. This conversation was not playing out exactly how he thought it would. I just couldn't tell why he was talking to me in the first place.

"But he left the force?" I asked.

"He more or less had to. We may have a small force here, but that just means less friendly coworkers when everyone knows you're in the wrong. That doesn't matter now, though. He's still out there free and taking on cases like some big shot."

"So why do you want me to know this? I have to live with him."

"That's exactly why," he said.

I heard the front door open and turned to see Mr. Paz standing just inside the lobby. He looked identical to when I saw him at the diner the night before. He smiled and nodded at me, then caught the officer's eye. Apparently, he didn't find it odd that I was at the station.

"Excuse me for a moment," Officer Neal said to me, walking over to Mr. Paz.

The two of them went outside, leaving me alone. I assumed that Mr. Paz had come to see if there was any word from the police about his missing son. I wanted to hear if there was too.

Officer Neal had been the last one to go through the door, and he hadn't closed it all the way. It was also apparent that the two men had only stepped out onto the front porch to talk. I stepped closer to the opening so I could hear what the men were saying.

"I haven't asked him about it yet. These things take time," said Officer Neal.

"What if we don't have time? How do we know if it will still work? We need at least one more day. I don't want to make things harder, but if anything gets in the way before—"

"I know. I'll find out and take care of it. Just make sure the note gets delivered."

"I will. What about the amount, though? Do you think it's too much?" asked Mr. Paz.

"Relax. Fifty is what will work. We've been over this. Now, I need to get back before we lose our best chance here."

I quickly stepped to where I had been on the other side of the lobby and pretended to be lost in thought as the officer stepped back inside.

"Sorry about that," he said. "You can imagine how difficult no news can be in cases like this. Poor man. I feel for both him and his wife. But, we are doing everything we can."

I thought about mentioning that interrogating me about my uncle was not exactly on point for an officer who should have been investigating a missing person.

The door opened again and I was surprised to see Cecil. He stopped when he saw me standing next to the officer.

"What's going on here?" he asked.

I didn't know whether he was talking to me or the officer so I didn't say anything.

"Nothing to concern yourself over," said Officer Neal.

"I'll decide whether or not I concern myself. Are you going to answer my question?"

"We were just talking," I said.

"I'm sure that's all it was," said Cecil. "Come on, Evan. We're getting out of here. Unless there's a reason why you're illegally detaining my nephew?" he spat at the officer.

"Everybody here is free to leave whenever they want and they know that."

Cecil snorted and let the door slam as I stepped past him.

"Do you want to tell me what was really going on?" he asked me.

We got into the rental car and I explained what had happened at the park. Cecil didn't seem mad. He stared at the center console, lost in thought.

"Why do you think Jeanne ran off?" I asked.

"I don't know," said Cecil. "Whatever the reason, I hope that she's okay and that Neal stays away from her. Away from you. Away from me."

"Me too."

I wanted to tell Cecil about the conversation between Mr. Paz and the officer. I didn't know if he would believe me though. I also didn't know if the conversation actually alluded to what I thought it did.

"How did your lead go?" I asked.

"So far, all I've got are a bunch of unconnected bits. That's okay. They may connect yet."

He started up the car.

"I may have something," I said. "I mean, I have something to tell you. I overheard Mr. Paz and Officer Neal discussing the case just now in front of the police station. They didn't know that I was listening. Sorry if that was wrong."

Cecil shifted the car back into park and leaned over.

"Are you serious? This may be exactly what I need. Quick, what did they say?"

I did my best to relay the conversation exactly as I had heard it.

"From the sound of it, they were talking about a ransom," Cecil said. "That's interesting. Are you positive that they mentioned delivering a note?"

"Yes," I said, "I remember that part of the conversation exactly. It just happened after all."

Cecil shifted the car into reverse again.

"Do you want to come with me to talk to Mrs. Paz? I want to make sure she isn't involved with this before anything serious happens. I get the sense she won't care if you're with me."

"What? Are you sure?"

Cecil smiled, and said, "If we're going to be living together, you're going to have to help me from time to time."

I couldn't believe my ears. I didn't know whether or not what we were doing was legal. I always thought you needed to be a member of law enforcement to do this kind of investigating. Of course, if what Officer Neal had told me was true, my uncle had been an officer at one point.

For a moment, I wanted to ask Cecil about whether or not the shooting story that Officer Neal had told me was true but reconsidered quickly because I didn't want to ruin his good mood.

We drove to one of the largest houses I had ever seen. It seemed out of place in the small town. Part of it looked like it had been built a long time ago with additions on either side of it. I counted 12 windows on the front side.

"Remember that you let me do the talking. If I ask you to leave, you go back to the car."

I nodded my head without argument. I was just happy to be with my uncle. I wanted to see more of what he did for a living.

We walked to the front door and rang the doorbell. It didn't sound like a standard doorbell. It continued on with chimes and bells and even a whistle at the end. I was impressed. A moment later, the door opened and I saw Mrs. Paz again. She looked like she had been crying.

"Do you have news?" she asked. "Have you found him?"

Cecil shook his head. He didn't apologize or try to make excuses. He just let the lack of news sink in for a moment.

"Why don't you come in?" she asked.

We entered the house and followed Mrs. Paz into a large room just off the entryway. We both sat down on a lengthy couch and she sat down across from us on a white chair.

"Why don't you tell me why you came," she said.

"I think that's a good idea," said Cecil. "I hope you don't mind that I brought Evan along."

"Not at all," she said.

"I've been asking a few questions around town this morning. Most of them haven't turned up anything about Paul's whereabouts. One thing I heard, however, has led me to believe that your son may be being held for ransom. Have you heard anything about that? It is unusual for the family not to be the first and possibly only person to hear."

"Ransom? No. I don't know what to think about that. Is that good? Is that bad?"

Cecil stared at Mrs. Paz. I couldn't read his face.

"I'm surprised you haven't heard about it," he finally said. "I'm afraid that my nephew just overheard your husband discussing it. Do you know why he might not tell you about something like this?"

"What? No. Unless... Are you saying he's involved? That wouldn't make sense. How can you demand a ransom from yourself?"

Mrs. Paz was crying once more.

"I'm afraid you're a little ahead of me," said Cecil. "I was only telling you what I had heard and asking you if you had heard the same. Should I be jumping to these conclusions about your husband with you?"

I don't know how Mrs. Paz would have answered that question. She never got the chance.

I heard the front door fly open and turned to see Mr. Paz standing in the entryway, a wicked smile on his face. It took me a moment to realize that this wasn't how a normal person entered a house. I stood up and saw that both Cecil and Mrs. Paz were already on their feet.

"Monty, what are you doing?" asked Mrs. Paz.

Mr. Paz either didn't hear her or chose to ignore her. He was staring at my uncle.

I gathered that he didn't come home to sit and relax; he came home because Cecil was close to uncovering the truth, and that couldn't happen.

"I take it you're not happy to see me," Cecil said. "And, I'm guessing by how quickly you came home that I am getting in the way of your plan. You're going to try to stop me now. That, or you're going to be smart enough to drop your weapon and talk this out."

I noticed for the first time that Mr. Paz was holding a metal baseball bat, partially concealed behind his leg. Cecil inched his way in front of me while keeping Mr. Paz's attention on himself.

"Don't give me that," said Mr. Paz. "I can't drop it. We both know me and Neal slipped up and there's only one option now. Your nephew overheard us and that's why you came straight here. You're going to try to send me away. I know you are. So, I only have one choice."

Mrs. Paz screamed.

Mr. Paz charged forward and raised the baseball bat, but he didn't have time to swing. Cecil had gotten to him first. The bat swept along the top of my uncle's shoulder and Cecil tackled Mr. Paz to the ground.

I was glad nobody had a gun.

"Get to the car!" he shouted.

I didn't move. I wasn't being brave. I had simply forgotten how to move.

My uncle attempted to pin Mr. Paz down but he was too quick, managing to escape.

As surprising to me as anybody, my body started to work again. I stepped forward and attempted to seize Mr. Paz. The baseball bat came quickly toward my left temple.

I ducked just in time.

Cecil worked his way around Mr. Paz while the baseball bat rose once more. Before it swung again, Cecil grabbed the crazed man from behind so that he was almost completely immobilized. Mr. Paz started to kick his feet.

"Get to the car!" my uncle shouted again.

I would have listened if it wasn't for Jeanne showing up at that exact moment. She stood in the entryway, watching as Mr. Paz fought against Cecil's grip.

"Get out of here!" I yelled.

She didn't listen.

I watched as she grabbed the end of the baseball bat and yanked it from Mr. Paz. He lunged at her but Cecil restrained him. The bat came down with a metallic thud and everything went silent once Mr. Paz hit the floor.

An hour later, I found myself sitting next to Jeanne on the Paz's lengthy couch. We had been instructed by my uncle to keep quiet and out of the way until things got sorted out. Red and blue siren lights danced along the walls while officers walked around the Paz's home. Jeanne had just barely finished explaining to me for the third time how she came to be at the Paz's front door just as she was needed.

"I told you. I was watching you since we got separated at the motel. I followed you back to the police station until your uncle came, then followed you here. When I saw Mr. Paz drive up and get out of his car with a baseball bat, I knew I needed to do something."

"Why didn't you say, 'Hi,' at the police station after Cecil picked me up?" I asked. "Why keep following?"

Jeanne sighed and answered the same way she had previously.

"Because I was still embarrassed for running away in the first place."

I stopped myself from asking any more follow-up questions. I was just glad we were safe.

"Ready to go?" my uncle said, stepping up to us. "Jeanne, let me give you a ride home."

Jeanne looked uncomfortable and said, "No thanks. My mom should be here soon."

"Then we will wait with you," Cecil said, sitting down on the couch next to me.

"Wait. Where is Mr. Paz?" I asked.

"I imagine in the backseat of a patrol car on his way to the city. The witness statements I prepared will help keep him locked up."

I wondered for how long.

"But why did he attack like that? I've never seen anything like it."

Cecil smiled and said, "I don't know if I have either. Usually, criminals wait until they're being arrested for sure to pull that kind of stunt. What I do know is he had been listening to our short conversation with Mrs. Paz, and he didn't like the guesses I was making.

"Jeanne, you saw him listening at the kitchen window, right?"

"Yes. But, how did you know?"

"Years of listening for what does and doesn't belong. When I heard the window slide up, I knew it was going to be an eventful evening. I just didn't know how eventful."

I was amazed and wanted to know more. I had questions that needed to be answered before I forgot.

"What about Paul? If his dad was holding him for ransom, isn't he still somewhere dangerous? And, how was that scheme supposed to work? That doesn't make sense at all."

"Paul was being kept in a large shipping container at one or Mr. Paz's businesses. That much was obvious from the documents we found in his car tonight. But, don't worry. Paul has since been reunited with his mother and they are on their way to Paul's grandmother's house for the next few days until they can figure out what to do next. Apparently, this house has been foreclosed on and they didn't even know."

"What do you mean?" I asked.

"To explain it as plainly as possible, I need to go back six months ago to when the bank started threatening Mr. Paz with foreclosure. All of his investments had dried up.

"I was at the bank yesterday morning solidifying my theory about the Paz's financial situation. The check that he wrote me for taking on this case in the first place bounced, which led me to investigate further."

"Wait," said Jeanne. "Now that you mention it, why did Mr. Paz hire you in the first place? You ruined his plan, right?"

"He didn't call me. Mrs. Paz did. She wasn't part of the scheme. By the time that her husband found out, I was already in town getting ready to meet with them. He had to play along and hope that I was too slow to ruin everything."

"But, we saw how that turned out," I said.

"Indeed. And since you both aren't asking, I'll just tell you that Officer Neal Scott was also in on this little money-making operation. In fact, he may have been the one to come up with it all in the first place."

"What? How?" Jeanne and I asked in unison.

Cecil smiled again and said, "Mr. Paz has friends in high places, which means he has friends in the police force too. When he realized that his whole life was about to crumble financially, he asked Neal for help. I don't know exactly what he asked for, but the outcome was the kidnapping and ransom plan that almost played out tonight.

"Granted, I don't know that if I had let things play out whether or not any of it would have worked anyway. The whole plan rested on Mr. Paz's ability to manipulate emotions. He was planning on using a typed ransom note as leverage to withdraw the last remaining locked funds from his only remaining account. The bank would not let those funds go normally, but people can be persuaded under unusual, high-pressure situations such as hostage-captor demands. That note was found in his car and will be stored as evidence."

"He was going to get the bank to give him money for a fake ransom?"

"Exactly."

I couldn't believe it.

"Did Neal get arrested?"

"Absolutely. He may even be in the same car as Monty."

An officer walked over to the three of us. He was followed by a short woman with black, curly hair. If I had thought about what Jeanne's mom might have looked like, she would be it.

"Let's go," said the woman.

Jeanne stood up.

Cecil motioned for me to get up as well. We followed them out and got into our own car.

The following morning, I found myself waiting on the train platform with Cecil. I had hoped that Jeanne would show up, but she hadn't.

"Is there time to go say goodbye?" I asked.

Cecil checked his wristwatch and shook his head. He was about to say something, but there was no need. The train came into view down the track. It entered the station slowly.

"We'll look her up the next time we're here," he finally said.

The doors opened and Cecil stepped on. I hesitated for a moment.

"I promise we'll come back to visit," he said once more.

I nodded my head and boarded the train. The door closed behind me as we took our seats. I considered how I had never actually met Paul, but that I had helped find him. I wondered what other adventures awaited me down the line.

Just as the train started to leave the station, I ran my hand across my jacket and felt a piece of paper inside one of the pockets. I unzipped it and pulled out a folded piece of stationary. I glanced up at Cecil, but he was staring out the window. I carefully unfolded the paper and read a short message.

I wanted to tell you this in person, but I couldn't find the right time. You may think that Cecil is your only family left, but that's not true. You have a half-brother. I've enclosed a photo. I'm sorry, but that's all I know right now. I'll keep in touch.

Your Friend,
Jeanne

Also Read...

Fracture After Dark

A Dragon, Some Whiskey, and People

The Morris Mysteries: The Complete Series

Missing: The Morris Mysteries #1

Murder: The Morris Mysteries #2

Mayhem: The Morris Mysteries #3

Mirage: The Morris Mysteries #4

About the Author

Shawn Jolley was born and raised in northern Utah near the Wasatch Mountain Range, a place now called Silicon Slopes by tech enthusiasts and hipsters. He grew up in a small suburban home in a small suburban neighborhood situated between two large farms and a miniature ranch. His first job was working as a farmhand for an excessively rich horse breeder.

Once housing developments cannibalized the surrounding farmland, he got a job at a small movie theater on Main Street that had seen one-too-many rat problems. From there, he obtained a job at Utah Valley University, worked his way through a creative writing degree, and graduated into an economy recovering from a global recession.

He wrote his first book, *Fracture After Dark*, a suspenseful young adult thriller that met with favorable reviews. A genre-crossing short story collection followed that, titled, *A Dragon, Some Whiskey, and People*, as well as a series of private-investigator novellas, *The Morris Mysteries*.

Jolley continues to write and publish fiction from his northern Utah residence. You can stay up-to-date with his future releases by visiting shawnjolley.com.